THE DYING GAME

A Novel

Asa Avdic

Translated by Rachel Willson-Broyles

PENGUIN BOOKS

PENGUIN BOOKS

An imprint of Penguin Random House LLC
375 Hudson Street
New York, New York 10014
penguin.com

Originally published in Swedish as *Isola* by Natur & Kultur, Stockholm.

LIBRARY OF CONGRESS CATALOGING-IN-PUBLICATION DATA

Names: Avdic, Asa, author. | Willson-Broyles, Rachel, translator.
Title: The dying game : a novel / Asa Avdic ; translated by Rachel
    Willson-Broyles.
Other titles: Isola. English
Description: New York : Penguin Books, 2017. | "Originally published in
    Swedish as Isola by Natur & Kultur, Stockholm"—Verso title page.
Identifiers: LCCN 2017000614 (print) | LCCN 2017018737 (ebook) |
    ISBN 9781524705640 (ebook) | ISBN 9780143131793 (paperback)
Subjects: LCSH: Women professional employees—Fiction. | Intelligence
    service—Fiction. | Psychological games—Fiction. | Psychological fiction. |
    BISAC: FICTION / Contemporary Women. | GSAFD: Mystery fiction.|
    Dystopias. | Suspense fiction.
Classification: LCC PT9877.1.V35 (ebook) | LCC PT9877.1.V35 I8613 2017
    (print) | DDC 839.73/8—dc23
LC record available at https://lccn.loc.gov/2017000614

Printed in the United States of America
10 9 8 7 6 5 4 3 2 1

Set in Dante

DESIGNED BY KATY RIEGEL

I looked at him. There was so much I wanted to ask him, so much I wanted to say; but somehow I knew there wasn't time and even if there was, that it was all, somehow, beside the point.

"Are you happy here?" I said at last.

He considered this for a moment. "Not particularly," he said. "But you're not very happy where you are, either."

The Secret History, Donna Tartt

"It's a two-man con," said Shadow.

"It's not a war at all, is it?"

American Gods, Neil Gaiman

PSUF Protectorate of Sweden under the Union of Friendship

See also: Sweden, Kingdom of Sweden

The Protectorate of Sweden under the Union of Friendship, in vernacular speech **The Protectorate of Sweden,**[6] is a country in the UF. Its independence is disputed. The country is recognized by 107 of the 193 UN states, among them the USA, but it is contested by the other protectorates in the Union of Friendship.[3][7][8][unreliable source?]

A first step toward the Union of Friendship was taken following the Wall Coup in 1989 and the unrest that ensued. Sweden and Finland have been under a state of martial law and the alliance of defense since 1992. Norway followed later on. On February 17, 1995, the parliament of the Protectorate of Sweden declared itself a full member of the Union of Friendship. The Western bloc does not accept this declaration and many UN countries still consider the Protectorate of Sweden an independent country. The Protectorate of Sweden has de facto and de jure control over its entire territory, but it is simultaneously subject to the common laws of the Union of Friendship, which preempt local statutes.[9] The International Court of Justice in The Hague does not regard the country's incorporation into the Union of Friendship to be a violation of international law.[10][11][12][13]

The Protectorate of Sweden is no longer a member of the UN and left the former European Communities before its dissolution.[14]

The Protectorate of Sweden is bordered to the east by the Protectorate of Finland under the Union of Friendship, to the west by the Protectorate of Norway, and to the southwest by Denmark, where the border has been closed since 1992. The capital city of the Protectorate of Sweden is Stockholm.

International Encyclopedia, 2016

THE DYING GAME

STOCKHOLM

THE PROTECTORATE OF SWEDEN

MARCH 2037

ANNA

ONE AFTERNOON, THE unit secretary came into my office.

"He wants to see you on the fourteenth floor of the Secretariat Building."

"Who does?"

"*He* wants to see you!"

The unit secretary looked extremely excited. Her thick glasses bobbed on the tip of her nose and she frantically shoved them back up, at which point they immediately slid down again. I could understand why she was so worked up. It was rare for those in the Secretariat Building to take an interest in our activities, much less in one of us personally. When I returned home from Kyzyl Kum for good, the Chairman had sent a bouquet of flowers to the office, with my name spelled wrong on the card, so I assumed they didn't care. Apparently I was mistaken. This made me feel both flattered and anxious. "When?"

"This afternoon."

She looked at my wrinkled shirt for one second too long

and appeared to be weighing something. "You have time to go home and change," she said, then turned on her heel and walked off so quickly that I didn't even have time to pretend I wasn't offended.

THREE HOURS LATER, I was plodding through biting wind and freezing rain across the courtyard to the Secretariat Building. Great sheets of half-frozen sleet were blowing straight sideways and whipping at my face, only to suddenly change directions and attack from the other side. It was one of those March days where everything is gray and wet and cold and the light is never more than a hope. There had been many such days that winter. It was mentioned each day on the news that we had never had so few hours of sunlight as during the past year. Maybe it was emissions, maybe it was climate change, maybe it was both. Or something even worse, but of course they didn't say that on the news. That was the sort of thing people talked about only when they were sure that no one else was listening.

The building towered up ahead of me as I ascended the stairs, as if I were walking into the maw of a giant whale, and the wind nearly hurled me through the doors. Inside the foyer, I signed in at the reception desk, received a visitor badge, was passed through various security doors, handed over my coat and purse to the guard, and was shown to an elevator. The walls and ceiling of the elevator were covered in smoke-colored mirrors, which made me feel painfully self-conscious in my brand-new jacket and bland, old-lady booties from the off-the-rack clothing chain closest to my office. The jacket fit well, but it was made of an itchy, tight material that made me start sweating even before I got off the elevator. My feet were damp and cold and my tights were sagging. I had put on makeup in the hopes of appearing less haggard than I felt, but I suspected that it had achieved the opposite effect. The rain had made my eye makeup run and washed nearly all the cheap powder from my cheeks; what was left was flaking over the eczema on the bridge of my nose and at my hairline. I felt out of place, like I was wearing a costume.

THE FIRST THING that struck me when I walked out of the elevator on the fourteenth floor was that the sound was different, more muffled. The floors were covered in thick, wall-to-wall carpeting, which made it nearly impossible to walk in heels without stumbling. This was a floor for men. Dark wood, chrome-plated steel, large green plants: scaled back, expensive. The walls, the floor, and the ceiling were imbued with power. An air-conditioning unit hummed nearby; it sounded like a distant helicopter. I didn't quite know what to do with myself; there was nowhere to sit, no art to pretend to study. A door opened and an elegant older woman came out. She said my name and asked me to follow her. I trailed her through the corridor and noticed that despite her high heels, she moved across the soft floor with confident, quick steps. She opened a door at the end of the corridor and let me into a conference room with a dizzying view.

"Coffee? Tea? Water?"

"Coffee, please, black."

She nodded and made a little gesture with her hand, as if to give me permission to take a seat, and then she left me on my own. There was a sucking sound as she closed the door behind her, as though a vacuum had just formed in the room. I found myself standing in the center of the room. Each detail, from the door handle to the baseboards, looked well planned. It felt like I was doing violence to the coordinated interior just by virtue of being in the room. Just as I was about to pull out a chair to sit down, the door opened again and the elegant secretary showed the Chairman in.

He was a tall man with thick hair and old acne scars on his face, and even though he wore an expensive suit, which must have been either imported or tailor-made, it looked oddly wrong on him, as if someone had dressed up a statue. I had met him once before when he came by for a tour of our unit. I remember the way we all stood lined up next to our desks, like orphans waiting to be adopted, as he walked around with the managers and inspected the work area and the staff. The mood had been tense and forced during his visit that time, and it felt more or less the same now. He took a few steps toward me and extended his large hand.

"Anna Francis, so wonderful to finally make your acquaintance!"

He looked at me, and as he did, I understood why it was that, despite all of his power, people often spoke of him so warmly. His expression was absolutely open and welcoming; it made you feel noticed, like you were the most important person in the whole world. As if he truly thought it was absolutely fantastic to meet *me*. I very nearly believed him.

"The pleasure is all mine," I managed to say.

"Please, sit!"

The Chairman waved toward the chairs at the round table, and as I took a seat he walked around the table and sat down across from me.

"First off, I would like to take the opportunity to thank you for your fantastic efforts in Kyzyl Kum. Splendid, simply splendid," he said with such emphasis that I wondered if our conversation was being recorded. He went on: "I hope you know how pleased we are with your work. The Minister sends greetings as well. Delighted ones, of course. We haven't had such a good reputation for many years. A humanitarian superpower and all of that. Just what the doctor ordered; we all think so. And of course we're glad to have been able to support you in your very, very important work, Anna."

"I'm very grateful for the opportunity," I heard myself saying, while at the same time I realized that this wasn't getting off to the best start for me. We were only a few minutes into our meeting and the Chairman had already gotten *me* to thank *him* for the opportunity to thoroughly destroy myself and my life for several years. He was clearly very clever. I started to wonder why I was really there. He leaned across the table.

"Anna, what I want to talk to you about is strictly confidential. What I am about to say must under no circumstances go beyond you and me."

He looked me straight in the eye as if to verify that I truly understood what he was saying. I did. I had spent enough time with the junta and the military in Kyzyl Kum to know that this meant, *If anything gets out, we'll know you are the leak,* so I nodded. Yes, I understood. He went on. "Anna, have you heard of the RAN project?"

I nodded again, feeling even more ill at ease. The RAN

project was one of those projects everyone had heard about, but no one really knew what it was. Judging by the massive web of secrecy surrounding it, it also wasn't the sort of thing you *wanted* to know about. One time in Kyzyl Kum, one of the soldiers had mentioned a case that had been taken on by the RAN group, but when I started asking follow-up questions he just looked troubled, maybe even scared, and changed the subject, so I let it go. There are some kinds of knowledge you don't necessarily want to be privy to.

"I know it exists, but I don't know what it is."

The Chairman shook his head disapprovingly. "Well, naturally, we would have preferred that neither you nor anyone else knew even that much."

He leaned a little farther across the table.

"Before I go on, Anna, I need to know: can I depend on your discretion? If not, this meeting is over."

I swallowed and considered my options. There weren't any.

"Of course," I said. "What is it about?"

The Chairman looked pleased and placed a folder on the table. *Where did that come from?* I thought in confusion. I hadn't noticed a briefcase, and the table had been empty when we entered the room.

"Anna, you're here today because I want to ask for your help. As you realize, it has to do with the RAN project. I won't burden you with too many details; only a limited number of us have insight into the group's work, and as it stands now . . ." The Chairman leaned back and sighed before going on: "As it stands now, the operative arm of the project has been beset by a defection. The simple fact is, we are one man—or woman—short."

The sentence hung in the air and my mouth went totally dry.

"I am very grateful for your faith in me, but I'm really not sure whether I'm . . ."

I cut myself off when I noticed the Chairman's astonished face. He stared at me for a few seconds with his eyebrows raised, and then he burst into loud, hearty laughter.

"No, I'm not suggesting that *you* should become part of the RAN group! No, dear Anna, I'd have to say we have other candidates with . . . well, different qualifications. But I could use your help during the recruiting phase."

I felt incredibly embarrassed, the way you do when you respond to a wave and then realize it was meant for someone standing behind you. I swallowed my shame as hard and fast as I could and tried to move on.

"How can I be of service?"

The Chairman clasped his hands in front of him.

"As I'm sure you understand, we are looking at several candidates right now, each one extremely qualified in their own way. And what we want to do now is test them in a high-pressure situation. A little field exercise, you could say. That's where you come in, Anna. You have a great deal of experience in confronting and evaluating people under extreme conditions. You are used to assessing strengths and weaknesses. You know how far people can go, and you also know when they're at the end of their rope. This knowledge of yours is quite unique, Anna. Not many people have it."

The flattery warmed me, even though I knew it was part of the strategy. I was supposed to feel indispensable and needed, and it was almost a little embarrassing that it worked even though I saw through it. I said nothing, waiting for him to continue.

"So what we were thinking is that we will carry out a little stress test. We'll toss our top candidates into an authentic situation in which you can evaluate them. See who shows leadership qualities, who thinks strategically, who is diplomatic, and who doesn't live up to expectations."

I still didn't understand what he was getting at.

"What is it you want me to do, more specifically?"

The Chairman gave a brilliant smile.

"Oh, it's really quite simple. I want you to play dead."

SO THAT WAS the Chairman's masterful plan, which he proceeded to lay out for me. A faked murder as a stress test. And this was how it would happen: the candidates for the position in the RAN project would be isolated on an island under the guise of participating in the first phase of recruiting, group exercises, and preparation in advance of the final tests. I would be presented as one of the candidates. The team would also include a doctor with experience in crisis management. Sometime during the first twenty-four hours, the doctor and I would stage my death ("At first we were thinking suicide, but I think we've settled on murder now," the Chairman said in a tone that suggested that he considered himself flexible and accommodating), and once I had been declared dead by the doctor I would turn to observing the other participants from what the Chairman called "a hidden position." My task would be to evaluate how the candidates handled my dramatic demise. Who took initiative, who thought about security, who was the first to come up with a theory about what had happened, and so on. After forty-eight hours, the exercise would be terminated, everyone would be brought home, and I would hand in a report about each of the candidates to the RAN project leadership. All contact would be carried out under the greatest discretion via the secretary of the RAN project. "What we're really interested in is your intuitive judgment," said the Chairman. "We can perform deeper analyses of the candidates later; for now, it's your gut feeling we want to hear about above all." I felt terribly uneasy when the Chairman was finally finished with his explanation.

"I'm sorry, but . . . doesn't this seem excessively cruel?"

I thought of all the executions, mock executions, and kidnappings I had seen in Kyzyl Kum and how they affected the people around them. Experiencing another person's death inevitably seemed to leave traces, whether or not it later became clear that the victim had survived. The Chairman gazed sagely at a point behind me as if the answer could be read there.

"Anna, I can assure you that it's not excessive cruelty guiding me here. The members of the RAN group are responsible for important things. Many lives. Placing a person who couldn't handle it in such a situation *would* be excessively cruel, both for the person in question and for the security of the Union. But I certainly understand how you feel, and to a certain extent you are right. Cruel, yes; excessively so, no. But I'm glad you are aware of how serious this is, because this is also why your assessment is so crucial. The fact of the matter is, we must know who can handle the pressure. All of the candidates will be offered all the support and help they require in the form of psychological expertise and crisis management. This goes for you as well, of course. And naturally, you will also receive appropriate financial compensation."

He named an amount that made me lose my footing for a second. I would never get anywhere near that sort of money, not even if I won the Union Lottery several times over.

"And besides the money—why would I want to do this?"

The Chairman gave a friendly smile.

"Well, Anna—be honest, what else would you do?"

Either he was an extremely skilled manipulator, or else he was taking a chance. Whichever it was, it worked. Because that was the thing: my job was meaningless, I couldn't return to Kyzyl Kum, and I was a stranger in my own family. With the kind of money the Chairman was offering, perhaps I could make a fresh start. Take a year off. Travel somewhere with my daughter, to a place where it was warm and calm and undemanding, try to build up a life again, fix what was broken. Or we could buy a house in one of the bedroom communities outside the city, a house with a garden. Siri could go to a good school; I could work in some local administration office, pick her up at school on time, bake buns, braid hair. I could *be* someone again. Part of my own life. I suddenly realized how terribly much I had lost in the past few years, and how close I was to losing absolutely everything. My throat tightened and I could feel a burning sensation behind my eyes. I swallowed and looked up at the ceiling to keep myself from crying; to do so there and then would have been disastrous.

The Chairman went on as if he had read my mind. "Anna," he said in a gentle voice, "I know things have been difficult for you. If you do this for me now, you have my word that you will never need to do anything else in your whole life. Not unless you want to."

I kept staring up at the molding on the ceiling. It was the exact same color as the wall; only the tiny shadow underneath revealed that it was there at all. The Chairman waited a second or two, as if to see if I was going to say something of my own volition. And then there it was: "And we would also consider forgetting those . . . unfortunate incidents in Kyzyl Kum. They were never really investigated, if I recall correctly?"

His tone was mild, but his words landed like blows. I should have known this was coming, and yet I was unprepared. I tried to get control of my facial features before I met the Chairman's eyes. We looked at each other for a few seconds, and then it was settled.

"I need to talk to my family."

"Of course."

"How long will the assignment itself take?"

"We leave at the end of the week. Then there will be two or three days max on the island."

"And after that?"

"Then you hand in your reports."

"And then I'm free?"

"Then you're free."

The Chairman rose. He opened the door for me and we walked into the hallway together.

"I need your answer by lunchtime tomorrow at the latest. My secretary will be in touch."

He shook my hand, squeezing until my knuckles creaked, and fixed his eyes on me one last time.

"I'm counting on you," he said.

Then he turned on his heel and vanished down the hallway

as I stood there watching the retreat of his large, rectangular back. Just as I stepped into the elevator it occurred to me that I had never been given any coffee.

I MET WITH the secretary of the RAN group a few days later to get the information I needed prior to the assignment. He was a small man, thin and short, with strangely bulging eyes and a large nose. He looked like he might tip over forward with eyes wide open at any moment. It was cold in his office, and it smelled like nicotine and tar, so I could tell that he ignored the no-smoking rule and snuck cigarettes by the window. He gripped my hand with an almost audacious strength when we shook, as if he wanted to yank it free and run off with it. The secretary introduced himself as Arvid Nordquist.

"Oh, like the coffee from the olden days?" I said, mostly to have something to say. He stared at me as if he had no idea what I was talking about. Instead he walked over to the short wall of the rectangular room, where he spent a long moment fiddling with the code to a large gray cabinet and took out a hefty stack of papers and folders, which he then dumped onto the table in front of me with a thud.

"Everything you will see in here is strictly confidential. The information must not leave the room, and you may not write down any notes, at least none that you take with you. If you need to leave the room to use the bathroom, you must lock the documents up again. Anything you remove from this room will be stored only in your mind; we can't risk any of these documents 'walking off.'" He made quotation marks in the air with his skinny fingers. His expression was accusatory, as if I were already guilty of unforgivable violations of confidentiality.

The following hours passed slowly and began with a run-through by the secretary. He showed me nautical charts, maps, and drawings of an island by the name of Isola, which was very small and situated all on its own at the very edge of the outer archipelago. The only way to reach it was by private boat. There were only two structures on the island: a boathouse and a main house. But the main house was a very unusual building. On the surface it looked perfectly normal: two stories and a basement that contained a medical station. But the house contained more than met the eye at first. There were small corridors sketched into the walls between every room; they were large enough for a person to stand in, and the secretary explained that there were tiny holes in each wall. A person could observe what was going on in the house through the walls.

"So that's why I was given this assignment, you couldn't find anyone else thin enough?"

It was meant to be a joke, but the secretary looked at me blankly and then continued to present the blueprints. A thought struck me:

"Wouldn't it be easier to use surveillance cameras than to sneak around inside the walls?"

The secretary shook his head. "We prefer not to retain any documentation from these sorts of assessments. Tapes can certainly be erased or locked up, but they can also be forgotten, purposely or not. They can be abused."

He pointed at a hatched area under the basement.

"And here, under the medical station, there's a subbasement: the Strategic Level. That's where you will spend nights and compile your reports when you're dead. You and the doctor are the only ones who will have access to that part of the house."

"Who's the doctor?"

The secretary smiled for the first time.

"Katerina Ivanovitch, medical doctor and an expert in trauma psychology at the College of Defense. I can tell you she is a very trusted person who has worked closely with the RAN project from the start. You are in very good company." Judging by the secretary's expression, he had greater faith in her than he did in me.

"The door to the Strategic Level is opened and closed with a code lock. You'll find the code in this envelope. You and the doctor will be the only ones with access to it. Be sure to memorize it well. Like I said, no notes." He rose from his chair.

"Now I'll leave you here with your homework. I'll come get you in a few hours." The secretary left the room. I sat down and stared at the nautical charts, the maps, the blueprints in front of me and wondered what I'd gotten myself into.

THE BEGINNING

IT'S ACTUALLY QUITE strange what can make us see another person, truly see them. Because to truly see is to acknowledge that you are in love, to suddenly catch sight of that other person there, across a room, as if it is the first time you have really seen this person, any person. When I truly saw Henry Fall for the first time, we had been working in the same unit for some time, and the strange thing was that it was just a tiny gesture that made me notice him.

We had been invited to the home of our boss, a young man with great ambitions who was said to be the right person to "streamline operations." The whole unit was there, all a little bit uncomfortable with and foreign to one another, a little more dressed up, a little more made up than usual, and with delicate glasses in hand instead of our usual old coffee mugs. Many people were wearing clothes that were brand-new, a little stiff. I noticed a price tag sticking out at the neck of our unit secretary, an older woman with helmet hair. Perhaps she still had the receipt in her wallet and intended to try to return the

garment the next day. And get her coupons back. I could picture her at the register, the blouse in a sweaty plastic bag, arguing over the receipt, complaining about the quality, the
size, a seam. The tired, heavily made-up face of the clerk. The
unit secretary would presumably succeed.

Before dinner itself, which was laid out in a spacious living
room with a view of the bay, we were served Rotkäppchen
from a chrome serving cart full of bottles. I stood there feeling annoyed at the fact that a little snot like our boss could
afford a luxury flat in one of the new buildings way out on
Lidingö, with a view of Karlsudd and the military base on
Tynningö, with a serving cart and Western-import booze; it
probably meant that he had family members high up (which,
in turn, would also serve as a welcome explanation for how he
got the job). Henry was standing, as he usually did, slightly on
the periphery of a conversation. Suddenly I saw him noncha-
lantly grab a bottle of expensive cognac, pour it into his glass,
drain it in big gulps, and then silently set the glass on the cart
as if it had never happened. It actually wasn't a particularly
charming action; in another person it might even have been
alarming, an indication of alcoholism, nervousness, weakness, poor upbringing. But in a person as controlled as Henry,
it turned into something else entirely: a hunger. When I saw
Henry gulp down that cognac, it struck me for the first time
that he might not be the man I thought he was, and that he
might pose a danger to me.

Once I started to observe Henry, I noticed more things. It
was like picking mushrooms in the forest. At first I saw nothing, then I saw something, then suddenly the whole ground
was full of them. The second thing I noticed about Henry was

his laugh. He was a man who laughed. That might not sound so remarkable, but most men don't. They smile mildly, maybe give a cough, maybe chuckle a little, but they don't laugh for real. Henry did, in a wide-open, unguarded way that didn't entirely fit with his subdued image. The longer we worked together, the more often I found myself trying to bring out that laugh, just so I could see him doubled over the desk or leaning back in his office chair with tears running down his face and his even white teeth exposed. That was a third thing: he had unusually lovely teeth.

Henry was actually a rather ordinary man. He attended to his work duties with zeal but a lack of originality. He didn't take risks. When it was his week for kitchen duty, the kitchen was immaculate. He wasn't closed off but nor was he open; he wouldn't share any personal information unless you asked a direct question. And then his response would be polite but brief. What he had done over the weekend, what he thought of the latest film, where he planned to go on vacation. He gave neither more nor less information than a response to the question required. Instead he often turned the conversation around to the person who had asked, not because he actually seemed very interested but out of politeness or maybe, as I eventually began to suspect, in order to avoid talking about himself. When colleagues sent invitations to birthdays, barbecues, beers after work, he almost always declined, politely and with perfectly plausible excuses. His aunt was having a birthday, he had booked the laundry room, he would be out of town, unfortunately. Next time. He was a man who never bothered anyone, thus no one bothered him back. Everyone at work was in agreement that Henry Fall was a pleasant person, but no one noticed when he wasn't there. Yet once I had started to observe him, it struck me that this friendly distance, this almost artful humbleness, was probably not a coincidence. It was of his own making, and that was how he wanted it.

His outward self didn't say much of note about him either. He looked like a small-town boy, one who grew up on a well-tended lawn behind white picket fences. Team sports and trading cards, summer camps with the Pioneers. He was slightly above average height and had angular shoulders, like someone who had played sports as a kid but had later given them up. Not overweight, but not thin either. Friendly eyes, brown hair. He didn't get his hair cut often enough, but his cheeks were clean shaven every morning. You could see a hint of freckles on the pale bridge of his nose, but it was impossible to determine whether his shoulders turned brown or pink in the summer sun. In the winter he always wore both hat and mittens. Sometimes he wore colorful socks with cartoon characters on them. You could imagine him owning a Santa tie but never wearing it. His voice was restrained and slightly creaky. He seemed like someone's neighbor, someone's childhood friend, someone you had met before but couldn't quite remember where. A man who vanishes into a crowd. If I hadn't seen him taking those big gulps of cognac, I probably never would have really noticed him.

I BEGAN TO gather information about him, what little there was. He never mentioned any children, no wife or girlfriend, so I assumed he lived alone. One evening I saw him on the platform in the company of a woman who didn't work in our unit. She was beautiful in a way that brought to mind the old upper class, chocolate-brown hair in an even pageboy and a coat with fur trim, and when she laughed she placed her hand on his arm in a way that made me think they were a couple, or had at least slept together. I tried to imagine them together, having passionate sex among crumpled sheets, but it was hard to picture it. The thought of Henry without his calm demeanor just made me feel embarrassed, but it was like it still got stuck in my head. I found that I often sat staring at his hands when we were at work, and in my loneliness I tried to imagine how they would feel on my body—but it was totally impossible to even picture a situation in which that might happen, and it made me feel idiotic instead of excited. It was too absurd. And yet I couldn't stop thinking about it.

SOME TIME AFTER I saw him drinking the cognac, we ended up on a project together. It was a standard assignment, nothing special, the kind of thing that just needed to be done. But as we began to work together, something happened that I think surprised us both: we functioned well together. What had started out as the blandest, most boring of work assignments suddenly became interesting, and as the weeks went on we spent more and more time alone together at the office, engaged in discussions about details that no one else cared about. There was an intuitive understanding between us that made it pleasant to be together. I found myself looking forward to those evenings when everyone else had gone home and the great sea of the office was dark, except for the island of fluorescent light where we sat together, with our coffee cups, our stacks of paper, and the plastic-wrapped pickle sandwiches we bought from a vending machine in the hall. It was as if Henry had crawled out of his shell and become more human, his sleeves rolled up over his elbows and his hair on end from running his hand through it, apparently unconsciously, time and again.

The work we did resulted in our unit being nominated for an award for excellent contribution to department service within our area of expertise, but when the award went to another unit I didn't think any more of it. For me, the big, unexpected prize was the discovery of Henry. But when I ran into Henry by the coffee machine the next day, I realized he wasn't at all satisfied with the results. When I mentioned the award, he looked grim, and his response was something short and sharp. He was, I suddenly realized, furious about our loss, in his very controlled and correct manner. That was when I learned that Henry, despite his quiet demeanor, was a competitive person.

A few days later we were invited out to dinner by our young boss, who wanted to take the opportunity to show us how much he appreciated our good work even if it hadn't won us any awards. "As far as I'm concerned, as your boss, you are all still winners," he wrote in his weekly newsletter when the restaurant dinner was announced. I suspected that he had plucked those phrases straight out of the department's leadership manual.

The dinner was held at one of the city's most buzzed-about

restaurants, one known for having imported pineapple on the menu and for almost never having power failures. On the other hand, the food was dry and expensive and the waiters were snooty. I sat beside Henry and felt a little uncomfortable about being with him in front of other people, as if we would reveal something private about ourselves just by sitting there and sharing awkward toasts to the project that hadn't won any awards, so I failed to notice how many times the stiff waiters refilled my glass. By the time dinner was half over, I realized I was drunk. Henry responded to my ever more incoherent and personal questions in a friendly but distant manner, and in a completely different tone from the one that had blossomed between us during our nights alone at the office. It was as if he were politely trying to put distance between us again, and instead of talking to me he spent the better part of the dinner interrogating a colleague of ours about the pros and cons of maintaining a compost heap in your yard. Regret rose in my chest even in the taxi on my way home: the feeling of having made a fool of myself without quite knowing how. Lone night wanderers plodded home or away across the Avenue of United Friends as snowflakes chased at their backs. I tipped the taxi driver far too generously, unlocked my apartment door, kicked off my shoes in the hall, stepped out of my clothes on the living room floor, and lay down on my bed, on top of the covers. Nausea rose in my throat like a sour chill and it felt like my bed was hurtling too fast through an invisible tunnel. I lay on my back, trying to concentrate on a point on the ceiling, and eventually I fell asleep without noticing. And then I dreamed about Henry. We were lying in a bed together, in our underwear, in a large white room with curtains fluttering at a blind window. It was understood that we would soon kiss, but things kept getting in the way. Time kept expanding and contracting. Suddenly a big party was taking place in the next room. People came in, searching for things; Henry went out to look for something too, and he did come back, but he got right back up again. "Soon," I thought in the dream, "soon he will kiss me." When my alarm clock woke me up, I had no idea where I was at first, but the moment I realized I was lying in my bed, my first reaction was an urge to claw my way back into the dream.

I performed my morning routines as if in a haze, showering, brushing my teeth, and getting dressed without any idea what I was doing. Every cell in my body felt like it wanted to flee, and on the commuter train to work I sat slightly hunched over my own body, as though someone had punched me in the stomach. It was a hangover and chemical regret; it was the feeling of not being one hundred percent sure what I had said to whom the night before; and as I sat there gazing out at the gray suburbs whizzing by the train window on my way to the department village while simultaneously scrutinizing each word and action I could recall from the night before, it struck me for the first time, in earnest, that I had probably fallen for Henry.

A FEW WEEKS later, my boss unexpectedly called me into his office and asked me to put together a "dream team," as he called it. We would carry out explorative studies and calculations in preparation for a potential aid mission to the Protectorate of Kyzyl Kum, on the border between Turkmenistan and Uzbekistan, an area that had been the responsibility of the Union of Friendship since Cold War II in the early 2000s. The more he told me, the more hopeless it seemed. Even the aid project itself, in the vague description, appeared almost unfeasible, and it sounded at least as difficult to come up with reasonable estimates of how much work, materials, and personnel would be needed, given the combination of ambiguous guidelines and strict budgetary limits. But even so, something made my knees quiver as he spoke. It was more a feeling I got than anything he actually said, that for once it might be possible to do something that meant something. Something good. It would take an awful lot of slaving away at a desk with various budgeting calculations, and it would take coordination among several notoriously poorly organized units in the involved authorities, and the time we had at our disposal was very limited. On the whole, it was an impossible task, but I couldn't shake the feeling that somewhere in there, under all the layers of bureaucracy and complications, was a glimmer of possibility. So I said yes, and I thoroughly enjoyed the sight of my boss's surprised face when, after making certain that I truly had the authority to handpick my team members, I accepted the assignment.

"As long as they agree to it," my boss said, squeezing my hand with a bewildered expression. It was obvious that he had expected a different reaction from me, perhaps rage, since he was clearly trying to kick me down a rung or two while pretending he was doing nothing of the sort. More debate, maybe; more resistance.

The first thing I did when the meeting was over was walk into the sea of cubicles on the hunt for Henry. We'd had lunch together a few times since finishing up our last project, but it was as if our secret language had fallen along the wayside once we were no longer working together, and I was happy to have been given the perfect excuse to try to reestablish our alliance. I found him in the hallway, and as I dragged him down to the cafeteria and began to tell him about the task, I saw a gleam come to life in his eyes too. It turned out that during his years in the military he had been trained in the type of calculation program we would need to use to get an overview, and that he would be a perfect fit for the project team. We spoke for a long time about how we might proceed, who in our unit might be a good fit, and how the project should be laid out, in terms of both sheer logistics and a time-line. And suddenly it felt like we were back in our bubble again. By the time we went our separate ways that evening, I felt relieved; for the first time I was absolutely certain that whatever it was made of, there was a bond between Henry and me, and we both felt it.

THE NEXT DAY when I got to work, I found an e-mail from Henry, written late the night before, in which he curtly in-formed me that it would not be possible for him to take part in the project after all because he considered his knowledge of the issues at hand to be far too elementary and inadequate. He wrote, ". . . therefore, unfortunately, I must back out, and I hope that this does not result in too much extra inconvenience for you. Best wishes." It was such a formal e-mail, like some-thing written by a stranger to kindly but firmly cancel a mag-azine subscription. An hour or so later, our unit secretary ventured into the cubicles with the message that Henry had come down with the flu and would not be in the office that day. He was back at work the next day, but he didn't mention a single word about the project or his strangely impersonal and distant e-mail. He continued to treat me politely and correctly. One month later, he quit our unit and started working way off in the F buildings, as the unit director for a program that evaluated rehabilitation. We parted on his last day with a quick hug, awkward and impersonal, and a vague promise to have lunch sometime in the future. It never happened, because he never got in touch. I saw him once in a while from a distance at the commuter train station, but I didn't speak to him again.

Not until I saw him on Isola.

THE PROJECT HENRY declined turned out—against all odds and completely unexpectedly—to be a success. Somehow, presumably mostly to show up my despised boss (and maybe Henry too), I managed to accomplish everything within the allotted time frame and budget, and with the desired outcome. As a result, I and some of my team got to visit Kyzyl Kum to make sure everything went according to plan when the aid project itself started up. Our visit was originally meant to be a one-time thing, but later on we were asked to return time and again, for longer and longer periods, and in the end I found myself running the entire aid project on-site; I was also in charge of all coordination with the military effort. When discord between the clans ramped up, the security situation deteriorated, and unrest spread in the area, we were suddenly the only humanitarian workers on the ground. The military was there too, of course, but the local population was afraid of them, and for good reason. So they turned to us, and instead of being the director of an aid station I was suddenly in charge of a refugee camp that grew with every passing day, a job I unfortunately had no idea how to handle. Nothing I'd ever done in my life up to that point had prepared me for it, this improbable onrush of desperate people who had nothing but the clothes on their backs. The reinforcements and help we had been promised never arrived, and then once it did arrive it was so lacking as to be insulting.

I tried to compensate for my lack of knowledge and all the other shortages by working as hard and as much as I possibly could. At first this meant all day, and eventually it was all night too. And it worked. It was as if I had found an undiscovered bank account inside myself, which until that point had just been sitting there full of enormous sums. I did things I never thought I could manage, making withdrawal after withdrawal from my inner funds, and by the time I discovered the cost of doing so it was too late. In the moment, there was no time for that sort of reflection. It was the end result that mattered. So I kept working, along with everyone else; we worked until our eyes couldn't focus any longer, and suddenly we discovered that in the distant view of others we had become heroes of some sort. Journalists began to travel down to see us; they took pictures, asked questions, and went back home again in their secure transports. Sometimes we were sent pages of newspapers in the unreliable mail, and in them we could read about our own spectacular feats, which felt surreal and ridiculous as we stood up to our knees in mud, trying to

explain to people why there was no food and why we couldn't
help them get away. But it just kept happening. We were given
honors and we received media attention. My young boss was
promoted to another unit, and I myself grew more and more
famous. Every time I came home it got worse. I was invited to
participate in TV and radio programs, first in my capacity as a
Kyzyl Kum expert, but as time went on the interest shifted to
me personally. One of the big state news portals designated
me one of the "Heroes of the Union." I received offers to come
prepare food with celebrity chefs on TV, have my living room
redone by celebrated interior decorators with horrid taste, sit
in prominent seats at large galas and party functions, walk on
red carpets. I always declined. The thought of becoming
someone everyone recognized terrified me, and it was always
a relief to return to the catastrophe, no matter how strange
that might seem.

IN THE END, something had to give. Of course. For many different reasons. And once it started to fall apart, it happened
fast. I was ordered to terminate my project and I left Kyzyl
Kum for good two years after I went there for the first time.
When I got back home, I was in very bad shape. I spent my
first month at home in the closed recovery unit of the veter-
ans' hospital. Later I was moved to more specialized rehab
units, and eventually I was discharged and was able to return
home, to my family and my desk job at the department. Then
came the melancholy, the pointlessness, and the shame. Because there I was, back again, in my safe country, in my comfortable home, with my stocked refrigerator. The people of

Kyzyl Kum were still there and I had let them down in so very many ways. I remembered a book I had read a long time before about how people who have been through tragedy are often struck by terrible feelings of guilt over having survived, which at the time had seemed preposterous. But now, in light of my time in Kyzyl Kum, it became perfectly understandable. It was as if I were not in the right. As if something had gone wrong somewhere, or maybe it was me, maybe I had cheated? When I first came home and was in the hospital, all I wanted to do was sleep, but once I was discharged from all the various steps of rehabilitation and was back to my everyday life again, I had more and more trouble sleeping. Kyzyl Kum was still there in my body. I was like a miner who could no longer get all the coal dust off her hands. The fear and uncertainty had become part of me. The cold nights, the fear, the whispering sounds from the dormitories, the explosions at night, sometimes far off, sometimes close by. I heard the rats scurrying, the people moving; I pulled my thin army blanket over me as if I were freezing, even though I was lying alone in my apartment under a warm down comforter. I often found myself sitting on the sofa at night, staring without seeing at TV programs about dangerous animals, wars, or crimes committed long ago. Black-and-white newsreels and slow documentaries that were broadcast when normal people were asleep. I often sat like that until the morning paper thudded through the mail slot at dawn. That was a sound I both feared and welcomed, a signal that this night, too, was lost, that I had officially failed once more, which meant I could go lie down and sleep dreamlessly for a few hours before my alarm clock rang and yanked me into yet another day.

# # #

SIRI CONTINUED TO live with Nour. There was nothing strange about this, and at the same time there was. Even back when Siri was born, Nour had surprised me by doing things I had never seen her do during my own childhood. Her first gift to Siri was a dress that looked like a cake for an oligarch's wedding, a gigantic, pink and white croque-en-bouche, with lace every which way. When I turned the dress inside out I noticed that it was dry-clean only, but when I pointed out the absurdity in giving a baby a dress that couldn't be machine-washed, Nour tossed her head in irritation.

"You really need to stop being so uptight, Anna," she said, taking a deep drag from her cigarillo, which she had lit in the hospital despite all the warning signs. "Let the girl have nice clothes, it's never killed anyone." This was pretty rich coming from a woman who had cut her own daughter's hair with kitchen shears and let her go around dressed in secondhand Pioneer clothing every day year after year, because they were "priceworthy, practical, and political," Nour's three catch-words when it came to my upbringing, back in the day. But if there was anything Nour was good at, it was forgetting. And I was grateful that she was taking any interest in Siri at all; from where I was standing this was not an automatic result of becoming a grandmother.

It soon turned out that Nour didn't just show interest in Siri, she truly loved her. And Siri loved her back. Her "Mommo" with the furrowed cheeks, black hair (Nour's hair had gone gray, maybe even white, years ago, but she continued to dye it), her hard pinches and rolled-up sleeves; Mommo who smelled like tobacco and patchouli shampoo, who rapped her crutch on the floor when she was angry, made ćevapčići while humming and smoking at the stove in her old apartment in the Olof Palme neighborhood, which had once been called Gamla Stan. Even before I went to Kyzyl Kum, Siri spent a lot of time there. Maybe too much, I sometimes thought in retrospect. Nour was the one who picked her up from the Pioneers' day care, brought Siri to her place, prepared food. I would go get her from Nour's around seven; when I worked late she would sleep over.

In time, Nour's office turned into Siri's bedroom. Like Nour herself, the piles of books and papers did something they'd never done during my own childhood: they moved aside and made space. A slow army of stuffed animals and toys, little dresses and floral sheets captured more and more territory in a clever pincer maneuver until the piles of books retreated and were crammed up along the wall. Eventually some of them even ended up in cardboard boxes up in the attic. So it wasn't strange at all that Nour should be the one to take care of Siri when I went away the first time. The strange part was what happened later: Siri never really came home again, and I didn't quite know how it ended up that way. I recall a passage from one of Nour's dusty old favorite novels that she had presumably forced me to read when I was younger, in which one of the main characters is asked how his financial ruin came about, and he responds, "Gradually and then suddenly." That's exactly how it happened when Siri moved in with Nour. The first time I returned home from Kyzyl Kum, I already knew I would be leaving again soon, so it seemed pointless to bring Siri home. And the next time it seemed pointless again. And again. And later, when I came home sick, it seemed not only pointless but also impossible. And in the end it seemed pointless for other, more difficult reasons. I watched them together, Siri and Nour, with their dark heads bent together, the small one and the larger one. They had started to belong together. When they walked outside, Nour held her crutch in one hand and Siri by the other, even though it must have been difficult and unsteady.

I had never experienced that side of Nour. Suddenly great care flowed out of her hands. They prepared food, braided hair, tucked in blankets, zipped zippers, tied shoes. And Siri always had one hand on her, in her hair, on her arm, against her cheek. When I saw them together I saw a closed, self-sustaining system, in which energy was transferred from one party to the other, in which nothing was really lacking. I had been away, they had been home; they made up one another's everyday lives, while I was the exception. It felt as if I were mostly a bother to them, as if they were both ashamed because they were supposed to love me but couldn't. So Siri stayed with Nour. I was the one who came for visits, twice a week. And even when we were all in the same room, it felt like I was observing them from the outside. They sat in a circle of light, leaning against one another, bent over a joint project that demanded their full attention. Part of me wanted to put out my hand and touch them, but I couldn't bring myself to do it. I was no longer part of my own family. They had become one thing; I had become another.

The person who gazed back out of the mirror at me these days was someone very like myself: a tall, thin, middle-aged woman, short hair that was no longer blond but gray, dressed in dark, practical clothes. Her face was gaunt, serious; perhaps it had once been pretty, or at least not completely off-putting, if it hadn't been for the hints of wrinkles, the red, stress-induced eczema, the dark shadows under her eyes. Those eyes were the problem. They were no longer mine. Someone else was staring at me out of the familiar eye sockets; someone was hiding in there, a person peering out of a black window, hidden in the darkness, impossible to see. I found myself wishing more and more often that I was back in the camp in Kyzyl Kum, even though that was the last place on earth I wanted to go. I was home, and yet I had never been more lost.

That was the shape I was in when I was offered the assignment.

STOCKHOLM

THE PROTECTORATE OF SWEDEN

MARCH 2037

THE EVENING BEFORE our departure, I went over to say good-bye to Nour and Siri. Nour's apartment was on a narrow street that was among the oldest in all of Stockholm. The Olof Palme neighborhood was almost the only one that had survived the demolition. There were even still cobblestones on some streets, and I was secretly glad that this part of the city had not been razed and straightened out, even if I would never say so out loud. Nour had been allowed to take over Grandpa's apartment when he moved back home to Bosnia, which had left the Union after the Balkan War. This was after they had started seriously building up the outer suburbs, which enjoyed express train service every five minutes. Life in the city suddenly seemed seedy and low status, and that was how we ended up with the peculiar reality in which almost the only people who lived in the beautiful flats in the old part of the city were immigrants like Grandpa. And now Nour.

I walked through the front door and up the narrow, uneven steps. The steps of the stone staircase were worn and sloped gently, like old bars of soap. How Nour managed to get up the stairs with her crutch was a mystery. I was late, as usual, and Nour opened the door with a stern expression.

"I hardly thought you would show up," she said as she let me into the hall.

"Why wouldn't I?"

I took off my shoes and placed them beside Siri's winter boots, which were arranged neatly under her jacket. Small black boots with white fur trim. They looked new and expensive. I thought about asking Nour how much they had cost and offering to pay, but I couldn't quite bring myself to do it. Nour walked to the kitchen without answering my question and began to clatter through the dishes as she called out something I couldn't hear.

"What?"

"She's already in bed. Go up and say good-bye before she falls asleep."

I walked into the apartment and up the stairs to Nour's old office. There had been many such offices throughout the years, in all the apartments we lived in, and I had never been allowed to enter them without permission. These days, there was a sign on the door drawn in crayon of a happy cat and flowers, on which Siri had printed her name in sprawling, multicolored letters. I knocked softly, and when no one answered I stepped in. Siri was tucked into bed, in her blue polka-dot sheets, and she was paging through a book I had given her about a bear who starts school. Surrounding her in bed were stuffed animals, staring blindly out of their button eyes, and on the wall above the bed was a picture of me and her together in Kyzyl Kum. Two identical smiles; her long dark hair beside mine, short and blond. On my first visit there, she and Nour had flown down to see me, back when my job was administrative. That was before the cold and the refugees, before the violence. There hadn't been any visits during my later trips. No more family photos.

I sat on the bed beside her. Her body stiffened immediately.

"Should I read to you?"

She shook her head, staring at me with eyes as big and round as a cat's. I hesitated for a moment, then reached out my hand and brushed her dark bangs off of her forehead. Her hair felt nice and a little coarse under my hand. She held her breath for a second, but then she rested her head against my side. I put my arm around her and pulled her against me. We sat there like that for a moment, both a touch uncomfortable, but still capturing the sudden closeness that I, at least, didn't want to disrupt. I stroked her cheeks. They were soft and smooth. Their childish roundness from the photo above the bed was starting to disappear, and in some brief moments you could glimpse the angularity and beauty she would likely develop as a teenager. Her skinny arms rested on the blanket, the book in her hands. When she was a baby, they had constantly encircled my fingers, her cheek against my breast, her heart against my own.

"You know I'm going away again?"

I felt her stiffen once more. She said nothing but gave a short nod.

"It's just for a few days this time, and then I'll come home again. And after that I'm going to stay home; I'm not going to go away anymore."

Her body was stiff and still, except for the fidgety movements of her hands, which were picking at a thread that had come loose from her duvet cover. I continued to stroke her cheek.

"And when I come home again, we can do tons of fun stuff. We can go to the sea again—would you like to do that?"

She still didn't respond. I could hear the forced tone of my voice, cheerful and ingratiating. Why would she want to go to the sea with me? She hardly knew me anymore.

"So, time to go to sleep, and we'll see each other again in a few days. Good night, my darling, sleep tight."

I took her book, tucked her in, kissed her on the cheek, and turned out the light. She was lying on her back, her face turned toward the wall. The contours of her thin body were barely visible under the billowy duvet. Just as I was on my way out of the darkened room, I heard her voice for the first time since I'd come in:

"Mom?"

"What is it, sweetie?"

"Are you coming back?"

I hesitated a second too long.

"Of course I'm coming back. Go to sleep now, honey."

As I walked down the stairs, I felt something tacky along my jawline, and only when I raised my hand to wipe it away did I realize it was my own tears.

I walked through the living room and stopped there for a moment. It wasn't just the building that felt old; Nour's entire home was like a piece of an old world. When I was little, she had decorated it with furniture from IKEA and Hellerau, just as the party recommended, but as the years went by and her personal enthusiasm for the party waned, the more her home began to look like Grandpa's. Photographs of old relatives instead of party leaders, Oriental carpets on the floor, old books on the shelves. And not just there—dusty books everywhere. Nour says that when Grandpa came here from Bosnia in the 1970s, when that country was still part of Yugoslavia, it wasn't unusual to see foreigners here. Nowadays you hardly ever saw them. Most of those who came here left the Baltic Sea area after the Wall Coup in 1989, after the dissidents tried to tear down the wall between East and West Germany, before the annexation. Nour and her home were a dying breed in this world. In some ways I was happy that Siri got to have them in her life, even though it might create problems for her in the future.

I walked into the kitchen and sat down on a chair at the table. Nour was still doing dishes, her back to me. Suddenly she put down her hands and stopped working, although she still hadn't turned around.

"She wonders what you're up to, you know."

"What do you mean?"

"Why you have to disappear all the time."

I felt the panic rising in my chest, the urge to defend myself. I sat without speaking for a moment. Then I said, "But she has you."

Nour turned around. There were dark circles under her eyes. It suddenly struck me that she was about to turn seventy. I had always considered her immortal, like someone who existed outside of time. She gave me a searching look, then turned to the cupboard and took out two glasses and a bottle of vodka, sat down across from me, placed the glasses in front of us, and filled each. She looked at me for a long time, as if she were trying to determine whether I would be receptive to what she wanted to say.

"Don't be mad," she said at last.

"About what?"

"About what I'm going to ask you."

"Well, doesn't that depend on what you're going to ask?"

"Don't brush this off with jokes; this is serious."

She wouldn't stop looking at me.

"Okay, ask away."

Nour lifted her glass, took a large, fast gulp, and put it down again.

"What I want to know is, are you coming back?"

"I'll be gone for two or three days, and then . . ."

Nour shook her head frantically.

"No, no, no, that's not what I mean. I mean *are you coming back?*"

I stared back at her until she looked away, turning her eyes to the dark window. Neither of us said anything for a long time. In the end, it was Nour who started to speak again, in a low voice: "There's a little girl lying up there who doesn't know whether she has a mom. And she doesn't talk about it, but it eats at her. I can see it, even if you don't."

"But she has you," I said tonelessly, once again, like a mantra. Nour stubbornly continued to gaze out the window.

"But the problem is, I'm not her mother. I'm *your* mother. And as it happens, I, too, want to know whether . . ." She stopped in the middle of her sentence. I saw her swallow.

"Know what?"

"Whether you're coming back. Whether you want to live."

A tear ran down Nour's cheek, and she didn't wipe it away.

"My little girl," she said quietly, still without looking at me. I couldn't tell whether she was talking about me or Siri. I emptied my glass in one gulp, my pulse pounding in my ears, then stood up and walked around to Nour, who was still sitting stiffly and looking out the window. I kissed her firmly on the head, where the white hair had begun to grow out under the dye, which made it look like she was wearing a wig.

"See you in a few days, Nour."

I walked into the hall, put on my coat and boots as fast as I possibly could, and ran down the stairs and out to the street, where I threw up in a trash can.

THE NEXT MORNING I left home before it was fully light out. A taxi picked me up on the sidewalk outside my apartment. Little snowflakes were dancing in the air as the taxi driver huffed and heaved my bags into the trunk. I was struck by the urge to turn around and take a picture of my building, as if I would be gone for a very long time.

The taxi driver drove out of the city and down to the large industrial wharves where the lake turned to sea; he wove around warehouses and stacks of containers before stopping at a pier with locked gates. He removed my bags from the trunk and placed them on the ground, but before I even had time to ask whether I was supposed to pay or sign a receipt he had hopped back into the taxi and driven off. I stood there alone, wondering what I should do, but then I saw a uniformed man approaching from the other side of the gate. Without a word, he unlocked the padlocks that fastened thick chains around the gates and let me in. As I looked around, I discovered that there was a surveillance camera mounted on one of the tall gateposts, and I assumed that was how they had learned of my arrival. The white snow had covered the ground like a thin layer of powdered sugar, and as we walked along the pier I turned around to look at my own footprints. They were already being covered by snow again.

Docked at the far end of the pier was a gray motorboat, military-style, and I recognized the thin silhouette of the secretary on the quay. Next to him stood a woman I assumed was the doctor, Katerina Ivanovitch. She was younger than me, younger than I'd expected, with blond hair in a simple bun and shiny dark eyes in an open face; she was wearing practical, casual clothing and had a backpack made of performance fabric hanging from one shoulder. Despite the raw, cold morning and the blurry dawn, she looked energetic, a Pioneer leader on her way to new adventures in the mountains, which made me even more conscious of the sleep- and stress-induced lines on my face. She shook my hand with a certain firmness when I introduced myself.

"Hi, Anna. My name is Katerina. Call me Katja."

She looked me straight in the eye as we met, and the way she repeated my name as I introduced myself indicated that she was used to inspiring rapid confidence in strangers. A type of secret handshake for doctors, psychologists, and priests. I wondered what sort of hold they had on her, considering that she had accepted this assignment.

The secretary put out his cigarette on the quay and pulled his gray coat around him.

"Well, I suppose it's time for us to go onboard, and we can hash out the details on the journey. It will take a few hours, so I suggest we try to get going as soon as possible."

⊞ ⊞ ⊞

THE SHIP HAD two rooms belowdecks. One was a lounge with brown leather sofas bolted to the walls, and beyond that was a cabin with narrow berths on top of one another. The secretary waved his hand, and Katja and I sat next to each other on one sofa and accepted the offer of coffee from a wall-mounted coffee machine. It tasted burned and had a strange flavor, and the paper cup felt thin, as though you had to finish your drink quickly lest the cup dissolve. But it was still coffee, and it was warm. I took a gulp of mine, way too large and too fast, and burned my tongue. Meanwhile the secretary blew into his cup with his thin lips, as if he were trying to play a misshapen pan flute. Then he set it down and started talking.

"I thought I would refresh your memories by going through the guidelines for your collaboration on the island. So what's going to happen is that you, Anna, will be introduced as one of the candidates for the position with the RAN group. Katja, however, will be presented as herself, a doctor, someone available as a resource on the island should anyone fall ill, for example, or have some sort of accident. That is also our excuse for having a medical station in the basement—that acute care can be given there, since a rescue evacuation would take time. After all, we don't want to appear irresponsible," he said, apparently unaware of the irony. "The stress test will last for forty-eight hours. In the middle of the night tonight, you, Anna, will be 'murdered.'" His fingers made air quotes. "Katja will anesthetize you and also give you a muscle relaxant, so that you won't move just by reflex. And Katja, you will later 'discover' the 'murder'"—he didn't even bother to lower his hands between words—"and send for one of the others to serve as a witness to what has occurred. We'll have to make sure the witness is thoroughly drugged at the time, so that he or she is not too observant. Then, Anna, you'll be placed in a chest freezer in the medical station before anyone else can examine you. The freezer will be sealed, and we'll say that Katja is the only one with the code. In reality, you can open it from the inside, both to get out to the medical station and down to the Strategic Level, and as soon as the effects of the medicine abate you can make your way through the hatch in the floor of the freezer and onto the Strategic Level. Then comes careful observation and evaluation, and when the time is up we will come ashore and pick up the participants as well as the two of you, and the participants will learn what they have been a part of on the boat on the way home; they will be cared for by our team. You, Anna, will give us the general rundown and recommend your candidate. Any questions?"

I cleared my throat before opening my mouth, afraid that my voice wouldn't quite work after the secretary's long speech; at the same time, I was debating how honest I could be. The secretary was not the Chairman, didn't have his power, even if he almost certainly reported directly to him. Perhaps I could allow myself a few critical questions after all.

"So you won't come ashore until forty-eight hours have passed, no matter what happens?"

"Correct."

"So what will happen if someone doesn't handle it very well? If someone breaks down?"

The secretary looked meaningfully at Katja, and she took over.

"In that event, there are a number of potential solutions we can turn to, so there's nothing to worry about."

"What sorts of solutions?"

Katja hesitated. "Pharmaceutical solutions, above all."

"So your plan is that we'll just drug anyone who has a nervous breakdown until the exercise is over? How well does that fit with your sense of medical ethics, Katja?"

Katja looked uncomfortable; a small wrinkle got stuck between her small dark eyes.

"That could be argued either way, of course, but nowadays there are extremely good, effective anti-anxiety medications that can be used in times of crisis, as you yourself should be well aware, given your time in Kyzyl Kum, if I've understood correctly?"

The question was posed in a broad sort of way, but it still made me feel slightly nauseated. It was clear that she knew more about me than I did about her. I decided to let the matter rest, so I shrugged.

"Well, I'm not the one in charge of medical care, so I'll leave that to you."

"How lovely," the secretary exclaimed. "After all, cooperation between the two of you is a prerequisite for the success of this experiment."

I couldn't help myself, even though I had just decided that it wasn't my problem.

"But what happens if it *doesn't* succeed?"

The secretary sighed with deep annoyance.

"We'll cross that bridge when we come to it. Which I'm

sure we won't. Naturally, we have made meticulous preparations and we know what we're doing. Now, I suggest that you
try to get a little rest; there might not be much of that to go
around in the next few days. There are cots in the berth if you
want to sleep; otherwise you're welcome to sit in here—there
are magazines and several TV channels."

I stood up and went into the berth, where there were four
made bunks. I crawled into the lower left-hand one, but I
couldn't fall asleep. At last I climbed back out of the bunk and
joined the secretary, who was hunched over a stack of papers.
When he saw me, he reflexively put his arm around them like
a schoolboy, as if I were trying to cheat off his test. I sat down
in front of the TV and found a channel that was showing all of
the old episodes of a TV show I'd liked when I was younger. It
was one of the few imported series that was still broadcast. In
the early 1990s, when there were still capitalist TV channels
and we weren't yet a full Union state, the series had been ridiculously popular among young people, and there had been an
outcry when the party decided it would be taken off the air. So
instead the state television company bought the rights, and
now it was almost tradition that it was always running on one
of the channels, year after year. Nour had told me, with poorly
disguised distaste, that American and British series had constantly been shown on TV before. Now this was almost the
only one left.

The secretary shook my shoulder, and not gently, in the
middle of a heartrending scene in which Ross and Rachel
break up again due to some far-fetched misunderstanding. I
hadn't heard him sneaking up behind me, so I jumped in
my seat.

"We'll be there in fifteen minutes; you might want to come up now."

I sat up straight, intending to stand, when a wave of dread, so strong it almost felt like dizziness, rushed through my body and held me down in my seat. Why, *why* had I accepted this assignment? Sure, I was used to unpleasantness from Kyzyl Kum, where situations had often ranged from unpredictable and threatening to flat-out terrifying, but I had never, ever wondered why I was there and what use I was. But I was wondering now. *How* had I allowed myself to be talked into this?

My brain started up the familiar defense program I had run through many times these last few days: I needed the money, I needed the work, and above all I wanted those reports from Kyzyl Kum to disappear. I didn't exactly have anything to lose, but I had a lot to gain. Repeating this a few times didn't completely ease my worry, but it did calm me down enough so that I could tie my shoes, pull my jacket around my shoulders, take my bags, and go up on deck.

KATJA WAS ALREADY standing at the railing, next to the secretary. I went to stand on her other side and zipped my jacket all the way to my lower lip. The wind off the gray sea was bitingly cold, and my hair was flying in all directions.

"There's Isola!" the secretary shouted, pointing at a dot on the horizon.

The dot slowly took shape, acquiring nuances and details, and as we approached I realized that my prejudices had led me to picture the place all wrong. In my imagination, the island looked threatening and militaristic. What lay before me was an undulating island in the archipelago, with something that looked like a rectory on the left-hand side. The building was neither particularly large nor impressive, but the cliffs below it fell sharply down into the water, which made the island look like a cake made of stone and grass. At the bottom there was a floating pier with a metal ladder that led up the cliff. As we got even closer, I realized that the pier was necessary to be able to dock the boat. The cliffs were taller and steeper than they appeared at first glance, and huge boulders jutted from the water even close to land. If not for the pier, it would have been impossible to approach the island, and I wondered how the first visitors had even managed to make landfall, much less build a house there.

We went ashore at the pier and the secretary immediately set out to climb the ladder that ran up the cliff wall. He seemed stressed.

"It would be great if we could hurry up a bit," he called back to us, in a shrill, strained voice, to keep the wind from stealing his words. "The other boat is on its way, and I want to show you the parts of the facility that only you will have access to."

I swallowed and tried not to look down as I climbed the vertical wall. By now it was raining instead of snowing—a misty, fine rain that made the rungs of the ladder slippery, and I cursed the worn soles of my tennis shoes as I watched Katja's deeply grooved hiking boots climb surefootedly up the rungs above my head. By the time we got to the top, the secretary had already started walking toward the house, and Katja and I followed obediently; her enthusiastic steps suggested summertime runs and cross-country skiing in the winter, while mine dragged like those of an obstinate teenage daughter. As we approached the house, I realized that my first impressions had led me astray as well. Despite its inoffensive facade, there was still something threatening about the place. Maybe it was because of the proportions. It looked overlarge. The stories seemed to be too far above one another; the windows seemed to sit too far apart. It occurred to me that this could be because of the gaps between the walls of each room, the ones that would make it possible for me to move around freely and observe everyone while they remained oblivious to the fact that I was watching them. I brushed my damp hair off of my forehead and walked faster, half jogging to catch up to Katja and the secretary.

"What was this place used for originally?"

"Evaluations," the secretary answered curtly.

"Evaluations of what?"

"Same as now. People in sensitive positions."

"So this house was built so you could spy on your own?"

He glared at me over his shoulder.

"There are always people who hide their weaknesses, and there are always times and places where that can affect others," he said. "Better to discover them before they do any harm. Which is what we're doing now."

He pointedly sped up to indicate that the conversation was over, toiling on up the hill, but I wouldn't give in.

"Do you really trust my judgment so much that you will be satisfied with whatever I have to say?"

"Well, it's not just you," the secretary said, casting a loving glance back at Katja Ivanovitch, who had tactfully fallen a few yards behind to avoid overhearing our conversation. "You will each be handing in a report," he went on, "and I'm sure that all in all, once we take both your viewpoints into consideration, we'll have a perfectly satisfactory amount of information upon which to base our decisions as we move forward in the recruitment process."

He walked even faster and put some distance between us as he hurried up to the house.

"This is where we'll place you when you're dead."

The secretary patted a boxlike chest freezer in a room inside the medical station in the basement, which, for what it's worth, really was like a small field hospital. Excellent for taking care of gashes, dislocated joints, bleeding, and abrasions. Less excellent for taking care of psychotic breaks due to stress. I recognized much of what stood on the shelves from the medical transports that used to come to Kyzyl Kum. Maybe a little too well. Various types of painkillers, anti-anxiety drugs, and sedatives were lined up on one shelf. I tore my eyes away as we were shown around, thinking about the "pharmaceutical solutions" Katja Ivanovitch had mentioned earlier.

My attention returned to the deep chest freezer when the secretary suddenly jumped into it and lay down flat on the bottom of it, his hands clasped over his chest. He looked like Nosferatu.

". . . And then all you have to do is this!"

The secretary pressed on something that looked like a refrigeration coil on the wall. Apparently it was a hidden button, because just then a hatch opened silently in the floor of the chest freezer at his feet. With a surprisingly nimble motion, he flipped onto his stomach and climbed down into the hole feetfirst.

"Okay, you can follow me!"

Katja and I looked at each other.

"Ladies first," I said, and Katja looked at me in confusion, but then she obediently climbed down. I followed her. And when I got to the next room, I gasped.

"Welcome to the Strategic Level," said the secretary.

IT WAS TRULY a remarkable place. The light was dim and yellowish, the way I imagine gaslights must have looked in the olden days. The furnishings and technology looked old too, like a telegraph station from the first half of the twentieth century. Dark wood, shiny copper, worn green leather in the details. The ceiling was a bit low, like in a submarine, and I found myself stooping although I didn't really need to. The air was raw and it smelled like a root cellar. The secretary flipped a breaker and several screens came to life. The images were black-and-white, grainy, and they displayed all the rooms in the house from cameras that appeared to be mounted just below the ceiling. I turned to him.

"I thought you said there weren't any cameras."

"These cameras aren't linked to recording equipment. They are, thank God, too old to be compatible with modern technology. Like I said, we don't want to take the risk of documenting anything. You can only see what is happening at any given moment, but the sound doesn't work and, honestly, the image quality isn't that great either. The cameras are mostly supplementary. In our experience, you will provide better observation if you do it directly."

"You mean by peeping through the walls?"

"By observing in a professional manner," the secretary answered reproachfully. "And don't worry about the electricity; even if there's a disruption up there, everything down here runs on its own generator."

He went to one corner of the room and pulled back a curtain. Behind it was a small galley. A refrigerator, a sink, and a small bunk bed, all within less than five square yards, so small it almost looked like it had been built for children. I thought of those who had been here before me. Days and nights without daylight, eyes on other people's lives. The documenting, the silence. The little galley was steeped in loneliness.

THE SECRETARY CONTINUED to show us around. A wall-mounted cupboard full of canned goods. A box of hurricane lamps and emergency flares. Mild painkillers and bandages. And then, next to the steps where we had descended, an abnormally narrow door of dark wood, like a storybook portal into another world.

"This is how you access the rest of the house." The secretary handed me a flashlight that gave a muted red glow, like a darkroom light, and waved me in; I walked in ahead of him. It was cramped, the ceiling low, and as I went up the steep staircase my head bumped the ceiling and my thighs brushed against the walls. The walls, floor, and ceiling were covered in a foamlike, sound-absorbing material, which my feet sank into and which sucked up all the noise I made when I moved.

There was something peculiar about moving perfectly silently. The secretary was right behind me. Suddenly I came to a curtain. I turned around and shone the red lamp directly into the secretary's face. He looked like a skull.

"A curtain means a new room," he said in a muffled voice. "If you feel the walls, you will find sliding hatches. Slide them aside, and you can look into the rooms. Just make sure to turn off your lamp first."

I shone the light on the wall, found a hatch at eye level, turned off the lamp, and pulled the hatch to the side.

I was staring straight into the parlor next to the grand staircase through two small holes. It was odd to stand there in the dense darkness that surrounded me and look into the other room, which was bathed in natural light. It made me feel like a ghost. The secretary spoke close to my ear: "There are audio loops in every room, so you can hear conversations quite well," he said. "But of course, if people start to whisper or talk over each other, it will be more difficult."

I turned on the lamp again and we ascended another steep set of stairs, up to the bedrooms. Only then did I realize that I would be able to see absolutely everything. There were peepholes into the bedrooms themselves, which contained beds and wardrobes, and there were even ones into the bathrooms.

"It's crucial for you to be able to observe them at all times," said the secretary, as if he had sensed my aversion to observing strangers in the bathroom. "People tend to feel more secure there. That's where they reveal themselves."

I shrugged in the darkness, as if to show him that I didn't care, even though the thought of spying on people as they sat on the toilet made me feel like a rat.

"Let's go back down. I've seen enough."

I gave him the lamp, he turned with a pirouette, and I followed the dull red cone of light down the stairs and back to the underground galley where I would be spending the next few days after I was murdered.

BACK DOWN IN the room, the secretary took out the floor plans I had seen in his office. This time the bedrooms were numbered from one to seven: six upstairs and one on the ground floor. This last one was reserved for the person who would be woken in the middle of the night to corroborate my death. There was still no list of names to indicate who would be staying in each room. We walked through the different steps of the plan one more time. Where I would be murdered and discovered (the kitchen), where I would be carried (the chest freezer), and here, where I would make my way later on. We were interrupted when the secretary's satellite phone began to buzz. He answered, gave a brief "mm-hmm," and then hung up.

"The others are on their way in now; we'll go down to meet them."

We made our way up the narrow set of stairs and up through the hatch, closing it carefully behind us, and walked through the front door and down to the edge of the cliff above the ladder and the pier. Below us we could see a boat, slightly larger than the one we arrived on, that had just docked at the pier. The first person to come up the ladder was the Chairman himself, clad in a statesmanlike navy blue coat and shiny dress shoes. They say that the Romans never learned the secret trick the Greeks used when they copied their architecture and temples: the Greeks built them with pillars that tapered at the top and with arched horizontal planes, which made the temples appear light, almost as if they were floating. The Romans built their temples the logical way, with straight lines, which made those temples look as if they might collapse in on themselves at any moment. That was how the Chairman looked as he stood there in his thick overcoat. Like a man about to be crushed under his own weight. The secretary immediately darted up to shake his hand in his usual energetic way, and they exchanged a few words. The Chairman gave both me and Katja a brief nod as he moved to stand beside us to make way for the others, who were climbing up after him.

THE FIRST PERSON to come up the ladder gave me a surprise. She was a woman in her midfifties, and even though I didn't know her, her face was very familiar. Franziska Scheele was one of the most famous TV hosts in the country; she worked for one of the many state channels, and her face had been on-screen for thousands of hours in our kitchens and living rooms. As far as I can recall, she had been the host of one of the country's most popular political programs; it ran on Sunday nights and she had probably interviewed every leading politician in the Union. She looked much frailer in real life than on TV—she was as tall and thin as a teenage boy and lovely in a worn sort of way, like an aging author. Her black hair was pulled back from her forehead and knotted in a severe chignon, just as she always had it on-screen, and she wore a long, dark green coat with a fur collar; it looked tailor-made, warm and dry, like it was meant for a hunt on the grounds of a manor. As she took her final step up the ladder, she extended a thin, ring-covered hand with well-manicured nails into the air, as if she took for granted that someone would storm forth and help her up the last step—which the secretary did.

The second person to come up was a man, also around Franziska Scheele's age. His clothing was meticulously expensive looking and casual: colorful sneakers, a cap, imported jeans, and some sort of down vest, like a prince consort from the old Western Europe. His face, too, looked familiar, although he was harder to place. I guessed that he was some sort of business executive; it seemed like I had seen his visage printed on the salmon-pink pages of the financial section of the daily papers.

The third man was old, over seventy, I guessed, and I found myself wondering what sort of position these people could possibly be competing for if a candidate who was past retirement age and could barely make it up the ladder was under consideration. But when the man shook my hand, he seemed like a younger person who had taken over an older person's body. His white hair and furrowed face carried years' worth of weight more than did his eyes, which were curious and clear. The eyes of a boy. It was the opposite with me, I had time to think. An old person looked out of my eye sockets.

Then came another woman, one I guessed to be about my own age. She appeared to have no trouble climbing up the ladder, and her handshake was firm and immediate. Neat and tidy, low-heeled shoes, a practical, short hairdo. I guessed she was some sort of director in the public sector, maybe not a higher-up, but not far from it either. And just after I had greeted her, the fifth newcomer and final participant in the experiment came up the last few rungs of the ladder and stepped onto the lawn. I gasped.

It was Henry.

HENRY

I NOTICED ANNA Francis long before she noticed me. I think
that's often the way it goes with her, that other people notice
her before she notices them. Some people are like that; it's like
the stuff they are made of is more potent than others. When
they enter a room, it's impossible to avoid looking at them.
Anna used to hurtle into work as if she were always late and
had to run. She always seemed to be absorbed in her own
thoughts, rooting around in her large bag, entangled in a coat
or scarf. She took the corridor with long strides; it was like
everyone else moved slowly in comparison to her. She always
seemed to be *on her way* somewhere, whether it was to the
morning meeting, the coffee machine, or the bathroom. Her
desk was like a fort of paper, folders, reports, and half-full coffee cups in various stages of moldiness. She herself sat in a hollow in the midst of it all, as though she wanted to barricade
herself off from the rest of the office. Her voice was sharp and
piercing, and everyone in the whole unit knew who she was,

but she wasn't exactly well liked. Although she was admittedly good at what she did, she was also surrounded by a reputation for being difficult. Many people, for example, found it annoying that she always had to ask a ton of critical questions at every meeting, usually when the meeting was nearly over and people were starting to shift in their chairs. It was like she couldn't stop herself from questioning things, whether or not it was an opportune time. That behavior worsened when we got a new boss who was young, uncertain, preoccupied by himself and his own career, and not really all that interested in what we were up to. The reasonable thing to do, of course, would be to pretend everything was fine and play along, but Anna made no secret of the fact that she thought he was an idiot. There were rumors in the unit that she had wanted the managerial job herself, but hadn't gotten it even though she was more competent. Whether that was true or not, the unit meetings began more and more to resemble informal trials, in which Anna played the part of self-appointed prosecutor and judge. There was something self-righteous about the way she scrutinized every single suggestion our boss came up with, as if she seriously believed that she was the only one who saw through him, as if it hadn't occurred to her that *everyone* thought he was a loser but considered it pointless, unnecessary, and unpleasant to fight it. But the more fruitless battles I watched her wage, in which all she did was make herself appear more and more impossible, the more I began to realize that she wasn't trying to put on airs—that was just how she was. Once I figured out how she functioned, I began to like her a little more. Although I suppose I still thought she was annoying.

# # #

I DON'T KNOW what it was that caused her to become interested in me, but it happened almost overnight. She went from barely even saying hello to me to suddenly seeking out my company, initiating short conversations at the coffee machine, and choosing the seat next to mine in the lunchroom. Several times I discovered her looking at me from across the room with an expression of inscrutable concentration, as though she thought she could find some sort of answer just by staring at me for long enough. Soon after I noticed this change, we were placed on the same project. I wasn't exactly enthusiastic; instead I imagined that she would poke holes in every idea with her endless, critical questions and we would never get anything done. But to my surprise I discovered that she was very easy to work with. The rumors of her extreme competence turned out to be accurate, and what's more, she was humble and pretty funny. That nervous energy that seemed to crackle around her became much less bothersome when it was put to good use, and she became easier to be around. More and more often, the two of us were the only ones left at work. It was no trouble for me to work overtime, but it was surprising that Anna could do so evening after evening. I knew she was a single parent with a young daughter, but I never asked her who took care of the child in the evenings, and she never brought it up herself. As we sat together and worked, each absorbed in our own task, I often took the opportunity to observe her. Her angular shoulders, her short blond hair with the long bangs that cast her cheeks in shadow, pale and greenish and sharp in the unflattering fluorescent light. Most people can feel it when you look at them, but Anna was unusual in that way; you could stare at her as long as you wanted and she wouldn't notice. Instead she allowed herself to be completely swallowed up by whatever was on the desk in front of her, and she seemed to be able to work indefinitely without losing concentration. But sometimes she would look up and fire off a smile that seemed to mean, *Isn't this nice, us sitting here and working?* And when, for once, I was the one who ended up in conflict with our insipid boss, she took my side with no reservations and no fuss and defended me not only to him but also to our whole group. When I thanked her for having my back, she just shrugged, as if it was no big deal for her. I assumed I had done something to earn her loyalty, but it bothered me a little that I didn't know exactly what.

ANOTHER THING THAT struck me after spending time with her was that she didn't appear to be particularly happy. What I had first taken as discontentment seemed to be rather more like sadness. One time I asked about her daughter's father, and something dark passed over her eyes; she grew evasive and responded curtly that he had never been in the picture. She also seemed to get a certain amount of help from her mom, who, as it happened, was a person most people talked about in whispers because she had been expelled from the party for disloyalty. Sometimes her mom called her at work, and you could tell straightaway from Anna's voice when it was her on the phone. She would always take the call in another room. When she came back, her lips would be pressed together and it would seldom take more than five minutes before she had a fit and chewed someone out. She often got drunker than everyone else at staff parties, a little tiresome and needy. I wasn't sure if she had a drinking problem or if she was just having a tough time.

WE STOPPED SPENDING time together after I left the unit. I would see her sometimes, waiting for a train into the city, always wearing jackets that didn't look warm enough, with her large bags and her blond hair on end, with that whistling wind about her, as if it were always blustery where she stood. But I never announced my presence. Things were a little tense between us after I jumped ship from her planning project, which, to be honest, I never should have gotten involved in discussing from the start. That was a misjudgment on my part. When she took me aside in the corridor to tell me about the project for the first time, my initial thought was that our boss had concocted it to get rid of her. Because it was hopeless. A suicide mission with no budget or reasonable goals. Endless amounts of calculation and soul-crushing paperwork. Anyone who had any professional pride at all would have brushed it off as impossible. Except for one, it turned out, and she was the very person who found it on her plate. As she tried to go into detail about all the problems that might arise, over a cup of coffee down in the staff cafeteria, her hands simultaneously and methodically shredding a paper napkin until only a pile of snowflakes was left on the brown plastic tray before her, her eyes lit up like a five-year-old who has just seen her very first Christmas tree.

"You realize, don't you, that this is presumably going to go straight to hell?" she said, flashing her broadest smile. Anna's appearance was strange that way. Sometimes she could look a little rough and ugly, like an old statue of Birger Jarl, but when she was enthusiastic about something she became truly striking. Sitting with her and listening as she planned great exploits was a little like being a kid and playing pretend, when it felt like anything could happen and everything was possible. Her enthusiasm was irresistible, and I didn't stop her, although I knew even as we sat there talking that the plans she was making for us would never become reality. Once we went our separate ways at the station, with warm farewells at our respective commuter trains, I began to feel uneasy, and later that evening I sent her an e-mail that said what I ought to have said from the start: that I had absolutely no intention of participating in an impossible project that had no resources. Of course, I didn't word it that directly at all; instead I came up with a reasonable excuse about how I didn't have enough experience in the matter, which wasn't true, but of course she couldn't know that. I assumed this was still less hurtful than telling the truth. In any case, the message must have been received, because she never brought it up with me again, but I noticed that it had still had an effect on her. She seemed to lose interest in me. She still engaged in friendly chatter at the coffee machine, but there were no more big smiles. She began to treat me with a polite distance. Presumably she was disappointed in me for not wanting to participate, and even though I knew I had made the right decision, her changed attitude made me feel uncomfortable. In some ways, it was a relief to get away from her when I was offered the job with the F Block, moved over there, and quit the old unit.

※ ※ ※

IT TURNED OUT, of course, that I had underestimated her. When she didn't mention the project again, I assumed she had abandoned it, but that wasn't the case. Not long after I left the unit, I learned that she had gone forward with it after all, and not only had she succeeded beyond expectations, she had also been given the go-ahead to travel to Kyzyl Kum herself. So just a few months after I settled into my new job, Anna and a small group of experts, clearly handpicked from other units, took off for the border between Turkmenistan and Uzbekistan. To the surprise of many, the project turned out to be a huge success. First there were rumblings about it internally, and then those started to trickle out. Suddenly, everyone knew who Anna Francis was and talked about her like they knew her personally, even people who I know had never met her. The more unrest there was in the region, the more Anna's aid project was discussed, in increasingly admiring terms. A journalist from one of the state news bureaus traveled down to do a lengthy report from the large refugee camp at Kyzyl Kum, where Anna was stationed as a coordinator. They followed her around the camp: she rode in jeeps, helped children, told off the military, handed out medicine. She was filmed from a distance as she, a lone woman, negotiated with a heavily armed guerrilla and filmed close-up as she gave an apple to a poor man. And just as when she asked annoying questions at our meetings, it was hard to say whether she was aware or unaware, whether she was playing a role and giving the journalists what they wanted or if she truly didn't know how perfectly she fit into their narrative. Her sharp features, blond hair, intense gaze, and peculiar, clueless earnestness made her look like an archangel, a wind-whipped tent city in the background, a scarf over her head so as not to provoke the local military. Half the documentary was made up of sequences in which Anna was staring out across a barren landscape with a grim little wrinkle between her eyes, as her sloppily wound scarf fluttered in the breeze. A quiet, admiring narrator went on and on about how dangerous it was in Kyzyl Kum, about how splendid the project was, and about Anna. Mostly about Anna. It was a heroic epic, pure and simple. You knew that the party must have loved it.

Suddenly, after that report, Anna Francis was pretty much everywhere. An evening paper included her as a potential choice in a survey called "Women Who Bear Up the Union: Vote for the most inspiring woman of the year," and quite a few people did vote for her. (Oddly enough, the winner was a princess who had inherited her meaningless title long ago.) I followed the coverage of Anna meticulously. I read everything that was written about her, watched every feature on TV, studied the angles of her face via all sorts of screens, searched her name far too many times. Certainly I was impressed with what she had accomplished, but there was more to it. I found myself hunting for flaws and shortcomings, searching for some sign that she had failed, angered someone, or at least taken a little heat in some opinion piece or editorial. I also discovered that I was spending a lot of time, mostly at night when I couldn't sleep, on pondering whether it had been right or wrong for me to dismiss her offer to participate. And even though I always ended up deciding that I had made the only reasonable choice, it still didn't feel great. I had made the right call and she had been wrong, based on all the known parameters, and yet in some strange way she was the one who won.

SOMETHING I'M SURE contributed to my interest in Anna Francis was that my own civil service career had come to a standstill since I left the unit. My new job did come with a more impressive title, a higher salary, and all of that, but my assignments turned out to be administrative, monotonous, rule-bound, and often flat-out boring. What had seemed like a step up, into a fancier room, had in fact been a horizontal move, a little farther down a long gray corridor. When I asked about the more stimulating assignments I had been promised, about increased responsibility and influence, my boss's eyes slid to the side and she gave a small, neutral smile which I assumed meant she didn't plan to do anything about it. The sense of having gotten stuck in life affected me to a surprising degree. In the past I had moved on up at a constant speed, receiving new opportunities and offers, within both military and civilian spheres. I had worked hard, and it had paid off. Suddenly this was no longer the case. Dissatisfaction spread through my body. First I started to gain weight, slowly, pound by pound, and in the mirror I could see the sharpness gradually vanishing from my facial features, which seemed to dissolve and become blurrier at the edges. My jawline began to melt into my neck; my neck softened into my shoulders. Without thinking about why this was actually happening, I began to take my car to work more and more often and stay home more often at night. This continued until I realized what was

going on. Then I got ahold of myself and started running.
Mile after mile, night after night, I wore holes in the pavement
in ever greater circles radiating from my home. Lonely nights
with loud music in my ears; dark, empty neighborhoods
where you came across only the occasional dog owner, teen-
agers sneaking cigarettes in groups of three at the edge of the
woods, and a car or two whose headlights shot a bolt of light
into the darkness between the streetlights. The pounds melted
away; my contours came back. I started watching what I ate,
reading recipes and studying nutrition; I bought healthy food
and made weekly menus. I weighed and measured myself in
every imaginable way, got a scale that calculated body fat,
measured my heart rate and the humidity, made diagrams until I could be confident that I was in better shape than ever,
even better than during my years in the military, and it all felt
great until I realized that it wasn't getting me anywhere. No
matter how much I ran, I was still stuck in the same spot in
my office in my gray corridor. Ever since my military career
ended, I had been completely focused on minimizing the risk
of doing anything that might demand my personal engage-
ment. I had avoided becoming too deeply involved with neigh-
bors and people at work by keeping my distance; I had avoided
having pets or a family or any other commitments that might
require my attention when I didn't feel like giving it. I earned
enough money to be able to pay a little extra (under the table)
for cleaning services and fresh fruit and ready-made food, my
own generator that would kick in when the power went out,
and, every now and then, liquor imported from the West. As
comfortable as possible, as few potential areas of conflict as
possible. I was independent, uncommitted; there were no

connections or demands to keep me from anything. I could work as late and as much as I wanted to, or spend an entire weekend on my hobbies, and no one would complain. I had always thought this was an ideal way to live life, but suddenly it appeared that it wasn't enough. It felt like someone had tricked me, but I didn't know who it could be.

THAT WAS WHEN the RAN project came calling. Even during the first conversation (with a snippy secretary with an expensive-sounding voice) it seemed to be pressing. Like a call I had been waiting for without knowing it. When Anna offered me a spot on her team I had refused; now I was witnessing her triumph from the boring sidelines and I was bound and determined not to make the same mistake again, should a new team come recruiting. So we set a time, and a few days later I stepped into the foyer of one of the city's few five-star restaurants. I was wearing my most expensive imported suit, which I hoped would make me look sufficiently respectable. The secretary received me in a private room at the restaurant, and he ordered for us both without even asking what I wanted to eat.

"Okay," said the secretary, "so you're interested."

This statement confused me, since I hardly had any idea what it was all about.

"Oh, absolutely. But of course I'm hoping to learn a little more during this meeting."

The secretary made a face that suggested he found this rather unnecessary, but then he took a breath and started talking.

"As I'm sure you understood on the phone, this is a one-time assignment. You will take part in a very sensitive recruitment process as an observer. I really can't say much more than that until you've agreed. This assignment will take place under great secrecy, in a remote place, in a closed group. It will involve hidden agents, and in some circumstances the situation will be . . . shall we say, strained? We want you there as a stabilizing factor, someone who can be of aid and support during critical phases of the operation, but also as someone who can intervene should the situation change. I have read your documents and I have full insight into your background in the military. We value your competence. It will be of use to you, and you will be of use to us."

I felt confused. I had expected an offer of a position in the Secretariat, maybe within the secret and operative arms of that enterprise. Instead, this vague one-time assignment was on the table. This was not at all what I had been hoping for.

"I'm sorry, but I don't quite understand what it is I'm going to do. What is this all about?"

The secretary took out an envelope and handed it to me. I looked at him curiously, and he nodded at the envelope.

"Open it."

I opened the envelope and removed a bundle of paper, by all appearances a personal dossier, and when I turned the bundle over, a familiar face stared back at me from a copy of a passport that was fastened at the top left-hand corner. It was Anna Francis.

ANNA

HENRY MUST HAVE read my expression of surprise there on the slope very rapidly, because when our eyes met he shook his head, the tiniest motion, yet still crystal clear. *Don't let on that you know me.* And as if to forestall any misunderstanding on my part, he stepped right up to me and introduced himself using his first and last name, as if we had never met before. I followed his lead, slightly paralyzed. My first impulse was to feel grateful. For reasons I couldn't put into words, it would have felt like exposing myself to the Chairman and the secretary if we'd made it clear that we already knew each other. But then I realized that, in all likelihood, they knew that we knew each other, since we had worked together in the past, and in their eyes our current actions must seem extremely odd. And then an even more nerve-wracking thought struck me. If they know that we know each other, and asked him to hide that fact—*then what is he doing here?*

\# \# \#

IN THE HALLWAY, the secretary handed out keys to our rooms. Mine was at the end of the second-floor hallway, and Katja's was next door. In my room was the generic bag I had been asked to pack for the sake of appearances, so that the stuff I left behind wouldn't arouse suspicion. My real bag, which mostly contained clothes and undergarments, was on the Strategic Level. I left my door cracked in case I might hear the others. The man who looked like a business executive had the room across from mine, and when the secretary entered his room to collect phones, computers, and anything else that could be used to make contact with the rest of the world, I heard him complaining loudly about the standard of his quarters. The secretary apologized meekly, in a tone completely different from the one he used to talk to me, for both the lacking standards and the inconvenience of being forced to give up one's personal valuables, and then he came across to my room. I handed over my normal, private phone.

"Assembly in the parlor in fifteen. Are you ready?" the secretary asked.

"Yes, I suppose I had better be, because now I don't have much choice in the matter, do I?"

The secretary didn't respond to my question. "Like I said, fifteen minutes." He closed the door behind him with a bang, and then I was alone in the room.

I had a hard time understanding what the business executive was complaining about. It wasn't extravagantly fancy, but it was elegant and clean and tidy, with materials and furniture that appeared simple and inoffensive, but upon closer inspection were of high quality. Sheepskin armchairs, fabrics from Svenskt Tenn, dainty little tables made of upmarket wood. Nothing was cheap or randomly selected. There was a refrigerator full of mineral water, nuts, chocolate, and small bottles of wine and spirits of familiar domestic and foreign brands. Every detail whispered the same, discreet message: class and money. Just one of these pieces would have been worth more than all the belongings of an entire family in Kyzyl Kum. Probably more than their entire house. I walked over to the window and looked out. Behind the house, the cliffs plunged straight down to the sea. The ground below wasn't even visible if I looked to the left, and to the right was a small beach that appeared to be protected in something like a ravine. A set of granite teeth protruded from the water farther out. I remembered that bay from the drawings of the island, and how the secretary had mentioned that it was sometimes possible to put in there with a boat, if the wind wasn't blowing. Otherwise you risked being wrecked on the cliffs. The island certainly was small. There weren't many places to go on it, not many places to hide. Aside from the fact that the whole house was full of hiding spots. I took off my wet tennis shoes and placed them in front of the fire, which was crackling in a fireplace along one of the short walls; then I lay down on the cream-colored bedspread and stared at the wall to try to figure out where the camera and peepholes were. There was a strip of dark, ornamented molding along the ceiling; it would be easy to conceal a small camera there. The peepholes were harder to find, but I found them at last: small, dark holes at the lower edge of the painting that hung on the wall. I rose from the bed, walked over to the wall, and peered into them, but all I saw was darkness. I pictured the secretary standing on the other side, looking back with his pale nocturnal-animal eyes. I lay back down on the bed, running my hands across the woven check pattern of the bedspread, following the lines under my hands with my fingertips and trying to think through the situation. It was concerning that Henry was on the island. It was one thing to withhold information from and play amateur theater in front of strangers; it was another thing entirely, and much more difficult, to do this to someone you knew. And most troubling of all: why was he there? Was he really one of the candidates? I had heard through colleagues in common that things were going well for him at his new job, but had he really been *so* successful that he was under consideration for the RAN group? I couldn't get my thoughts in order, and the more I thought about it the more anxious I became, so I got up off the bed, found a pair of acceptable shoes in my bag, ran a brush through my hair, left the room, and went down to the parlor.

MOST OF THE group had already congregated there. Franziska Scheele was standing in one corner and conversing with the man from the room across from mine. In the other corner, the older man was sitting on a sofa and talking to Katja Ivanovitch. Henry was sitting on a chair alongside them, nodding in interest. He didn't even raise his eyes when I entered the room. I stopped in the doorway and looked at the people gathered there. My gaze moved on, searching the walls; I tried to locate the place where I had so recently been standing and observing the room from the gap between the walls. I heard steps on the stairs behind me, and when I turned around I saw the secretary and the Chairman coming down the stairs together, chatting with the woman who was about my age. She slipped farther into the room as the Chairman and the secretary went to stand in the center, and the conversations around them immediately stopped as all eyes turned to them. The Chairman cleared his throat.

"A warm welcome to all of you! On behalf of the Minister I want to say how happy we are that you have all agreed to come here and take part in the first step of this recruitment process. In just a moment, I will go through the schedule, but before I do I want to ask something of you: do not discuss the reason you are here with each other! This might sound strange, but I assure you there are good reasons for this. *Absolute secrecy* is crucial to the position for which you are all here, so you must simply take me at my word: no discussions about the assignment."

He allowed his trusting eyes to rest on each one of us, as if to confirm this agreement, before going on: "Aside from that, you are of course free to get to know each other as much as you want. You're all colorful people with lots to say, and I believe that you will enjoy one another's company. So I thought we could begin with a round of introductions, but I'll keep it short and you can fill in the blanks yourselves at the dinner table this evening."

The Chairman turned expectantly to the secretary, who took the floor:

"So, here we have someone who hardly needs an introduction, since you've all seen her on TV. Welcome, Franziska Scheele!"

Franziska took a small step forward and aimed a regal smile at everyone and no one in the room, perfectly comfortable with being the center of attention.

The secretary spent another moment running through her virtues and merits, and then, when he moved on to introduce the man in the room across from mine, it seemed incomprehensible that I hadn't been able to place him. Jon von Post was one of the richest people in the country; he had turned his cheap plastic furniture business into one of the largest and most profitable in Sweden. A few years earlier, he had been on all the "most successful," "most admired," and simply "richest" lists in all the papers. But then, somewhat unexpectedly, he had stepped down from most of his ventures and as far as I was aware he was currently only on a board or two. There had been rumors of some sort of scandal, and now that I saw him it didn't seem at all unlikely. He looked exhausted under his expensive clothing and his tan, and he must have gained fifty pounds since he was last on all the front pages. At least twenty of those seemed to have settled in his face, which was an alarming shade of purplish red. He raised his hand in a restrained wave, as if someone had just allowed him to merge into traffic.

"And then we have Katerina Ivanovich," the secretary continued. "She is the only one of you who isn't here *for* the job but *on* the job, you might say. She is here for your sake; you'll be spending a few days here, after all, thoroughly isolated from the outside world . . ."

"*I* simply cannot understand why this isolation is necessary," Franziska Scheele broke in, with the authority of someone who has spent decades being paid to interrupt others.

The secretary shot a nervous look at the Chairman, who immediately took over.

"My dear Franziska, you know that we value your opinions, but may I ask you to trust us this one time? For my sake, if nothing else?"

The Chairman threw out his hands and gave Franziska Scheele a charming smile, and once again I thought about how clever he was when it came to knowing exactly who needed what. He had just managed to let her know that they both knew it was ridiculous that she should have to play summer camp with other adults, but those were the rules, and both of them would simply have to submit to this charade. And it worked. Franziska shrugged slightly, shot him a gracious glance, and acquiesced. The secretary went on to introduce Katja: "As I mentioned, it is for everyone's safety that we have a doctor on-site. There is a fully equipped medical station in the basement, where we also keep our only communication radio. We will strive to solve any problems that arise here on the island, but if urgent medical care is the only option, Katerina will certainly have the ability to call for assistance. But it's not as if you're going to be spending your time mountain climbing, so . . . still, let me say that Katerina Ivanovitch has been one of our most trusted colleagues and has been working closely with the RAN project from the very start."

Katja looked embarrassed as the secretary sang her praises. She didn't seem nearly as comfortable in the spotlight as the two previous participants had been.

The secretary then turned to introducing Colonel Per Olof Ehnmark. His list of accomplishments went on for quite some time: counterintelligence during both the first and second Cold Wars, international work; he had been inducted into all sorts of orders. I listened with half an ear; instead I was on the lookout for signs of what the secretary had mentioned about him before, now that I knew he was the one staying in the room here on the ground floor. So he was the one who would eventually find me dead, twelve hours from now.

"And then there's Henry Fall," the secretary said suddenly, yanking me from my thoughts.

"His work on psychological strategy has been positively invaluable within our own organization."

Henry flashed his small, neutral smile as the secretary talked about his most recent accomplishments. Now that everyone else was also looking at Henry, I could allow myself to study him. It had been more than two years since I'd last seen him. He looked the same, possibly with a little more gray in his hair and darker rings under his eyes. The secretary cleared his throat and jumped back in.

"Last but not least, perhaps some of you recognize Anna Francis."

He turned to look at me, and I stared down at the carpet as the secretary bragged about my invaluable efforts for the Union in Kyzyl Kum. I suppose I was the only one who thought his voice sounded like it was dripping with sarcasm the whole time. When he was done, I looked up to see how the others would react. I met the colonel's eyes, which were warm and friendly, but Franziska Scheele pointedly turned away when I looked at her. Henry was gazing attentively at the secretary, who clapped his hands together.

"And with that, I think we're finished."

"No, not quite."

Everyone turned to look over at the sofa, where the middle-aged woman in practical shoes had stood up. "Perhaps I should introduce myself, if you've forgotten me? My name is Lotte Colliander. Or am I no longer considered part of this group? Maybe I should turn around and go back home?" She gave a laugh, but it sounded like a bark.

The secretary looked helplessly at the Chairman, and then the two of them fell all over themselves with excuses and apologies. Of course she shouldn't go home, of course they were mortified at having skipped over her during introductions. Lotte Colliander tried to appear unmoved, as if it was no big deal, but the red blotches on her neck told me that she was as angry as she was demeaned. Her list of merits was certainly nothing to sneeze at: an expert manager and recruiter, director of HR for a long line of large firms, marathoner; she had double doctorates in business economics and psychology; she was also ranking military. I had never heard of anyone who seemed to be so good at pretty much everything.

"And with that, I hope you will plan to stay and take part in these initial days, and that you can forgive my secretary, who can sometimes be a little quick on the draw," the Chairman concluded. Behind him, the secretary gave a start as if he had been struck.

Lotte Colliander nodded and sat back down without another word, but as soon as the Chairman took his eyes from her she defensively crossed her arms over her chest.

"Now let's turn to a brief run-through of the next few days."

The secretary reached for a stack of black folders labeled

with names, and he began to hand them out as the Chairman continued speaking.

"Everything you need to know is in the folders you are holding right now. They are personal, so don't leave them lying around the house. Tomorrow you will be divided into groups to take part in certain exercises, most of which are academic in nature, but some are a little more . . . hands-on, you might say? You can read on for more detailed information. You may spend the rest of today getting to know each other, which will be to your advantage in tomorrow's activities, so make the most of the opportunity. You will eat dinner together this evening, and there is food and drink in the kitchen on this level as well as in the adjoining wine cellar. You'll also find food for the coming days in the kitchen, and I assure you that we have really spoiled you. There is no reason for anyone to leave hungry, but you will have to handle the preparation on your own—consider it a teamwork exercise! And now"— the Chairman turned to the secretary—"it's time for us to head back to the mainland."

I DIDN'T ACCOMPANY them down to the pier as the others did; instead I remained in the parlor. Through the window I watched the Chairman, along with Franziska Scheele and Jon von Post, march down to the ladder that led to the pier. From what little I'd seen of them so far, I assumed they were still complaining about the arrangements. Franziska was tripping along on her black high-heeled bootees, and it seemed like the wind might catch hold of her at any moment, lifting her up and carrying her off across the sea. After the first group came the secretary and Katja. The colonel and the hypersensitive Lotte from HR were nowhere to be seen.

"So. You're here."

I hadn't heard him coming up behind me. I reflexively turned around. Henry was looking at me with his usual neutral expression.

"You, too, it's been a long time! How are you?"

Henry ignored my pleasantries.

"I don't think we should let the others know that we know each other." He stuck his hands in his trouser pockets and looked out the window behind me, his face still expressionless. He was speaking in a casual voice, as if we were just chatting.

"Why not?"

"It gives us an advantage, don't you think?"

"What do you mean?"

Henry chuckled with his even white teeth and turned to me.

"Haven't you ever played strategy games? Secret alliances are the alpha and omega."

"So the two of us are going to be in a secret alliance?"

"I think we should." Henry looked me straight in the eye.

Once when I was little, I received a postcard from Nour, a colorful card with a holographic surface that showed an empty deck chair on a beach. When you moved the card just a bit, you could suddenly see a happy cat in sunglasses sitting in the chair, one paw lifted in a cheerful greeting. Henry was like one of those cards: a slight shift revealed something completely different, something more unruly, something that was there only if you happened to glance at it at the right moment, from the right angle. And just as in the past, when we worked together and he occasionally showed a glimpse of his secret self, a small butterfly unfurled its wings in my chest.

"Although," Henry said, turning back to the window, "perhaps you don't trust me?"

My mouth went dry and I stood there without saying anything for a moment, wondering how best to answer that question.

"No," I said after a few seconds. "No, I trust you."

"So then we have our secret alliance," Henry said, still in the same casual tone, as if he himself wasn't sure whether or not he was joking.

"Okay," I said, putting out my pinkie. He laughed, gave me a searching look, and then put out his own pinkie. We rather solemnly pinkie swore our new pact, and then he put his right hand back in his pocket and continued to gaze out the window without another word. I remained there beside him, gazing out as well, and thought of all the things I would never be able to tell him. At last I couldn't help but ask:

"So what does this secret pact mean?"

Henry continued to stare out at the gray sea, where we could now see the Chairman and the secretary's boat leaving land and turning homeward again.

"We'll see," he said. "We'll see."

I EXCUSED MYSELF and hurried back to my room. Once I got there, I lay down on my bed with my shoes on, staring at the ceiling. All at once, everything was much more muddled than I had expected. It seemed like the safest option would be to stay away from Henry, but that was also the most difficult plan, and maybe not even the smartest. There was some truth to what he said, that this seemed to be a situation in which a person might need allies, and it was best to play along in order to be believable as a participant. But in addition, there was something about him that made me act like an attention-starved child dancing around with her pants on her head in order to be seen. I realized that it had been this way with Henry ever since that strange e-mail. Every time I spoke to him I began to analyze and criticize everything I had said and done. Had I sounded angry? Did I look too happy? Did I talk too much? Or too little? I had lost the ability to act normal around him, because I no longer knew how he viewed me. Maybe I never really had known and maybe that was why I couldn't stop thinking about him.

I reached for the folder I had received from the secretary and opened it. It contained forty sheets of totally blank paper. I stared at them for a while and wondered what could possibly have been in the other guests' folders. Then I took a pen out of my bag and spent a few minutes writing down everything I had learned from the preliminary materials, which the secretary had forced me to memorize. And then I added my own observations from the afternoon's meeting. I embellished all I remembered with as much detail as I possibly could—tones of voice, glances, and my own thoughts on what little had happened so far—to make it all stick in my memory. As I worked, I realized two things. The first was how disparate this selection of people truly was. I had reflected upon this earlier as well, that it was an odd group, but now it hit me full force. Neither the Chairman nor the secretary had let a single word slip about what position they were recruiting for, and what it involved, but it was hard to imagine any position in the world that all of these people might be considered for. A TV host, a former military man, a business executive, a marathon-running HR star . . . then it struck me that there might in fact be a common denominator. They were all used to being in control, and controlling others. And with that, I could see how Henry fit in as well. This led me to my second insight: there had not been any information about Henry in the reading material I had seen in the secretary's office. None of the information I had received fit in with his profile. Thus I knew neither more nor less about him than I had earlier, which was certainly a problem, but more than anything else I wondered once again what this meant. Had he been added later? Was there any other explanation? Why hadn't I been informed about all of the participants? It made me feel extremely uneasy. At the very bottom of my handwritten document on Henry I wrote, "WHO IS HE? WHY IS HE HERE?" and underlined it with thick strokes.

I read through what I had written about each of them several times before burning the papers in the fireplace. When only ashes remained, I swept them up and flushed them down the toilet. Then I wiped the hearth clean. The secretary had been very clear about this: there must be no traces that could put the classified nature of the operation at risk.

HENRY

WHEN I CAUGHT sight of Anna on the frozen brown lawn in front of the house, it gave me a shock. She appeared to have aged ten years since we last saw each other. From thin to emaciated, from pale to transparent. Her skin seemed to strain across her skull, and what used to be sharp features were now more like gouges. It was clear that the project in Kyzyl Kum had been no vacation. On the contrary, it seemed to have cost her a great deal. And it wasn't just that she looked exhausted, it was that she looked *destroyed*, in a way that was rather ghastly.

To judge by the expression on her face, she clearly was not prepared for me to show up, but somehow I got her to understand that we should not reveal our acquaintance, because in a split second she arranged her features and greeted me formally. I squeezed her thin, cold hand, hardly more than a bundle of dry twigs, and exchanged a few polite phrases. I noticed the secretary registering this little scene out of the corner of his eye. Anna somehow managed to linger in a perfectly natural way, so that she was the last one up to the house, and it was hard to keep myself from turning my head and looking at her as I dragged my suitcase behind me. The house looked as unwelcoming and imposing as always, and as I approached its great bulk a shiver ran down my spine. I pretended to have trouble with my suitcase on the stairs, and I was able to turn around and throw a glance backward as I wrestled with it. The sky and the sea blurred together in varied, heavy shades of gray, full of ripples, wisps, and haze. Down by the pier, the boat was bobbing on the surf with uneven little jumps. Whoever had docked the boat had done so in an idiotic location that caused it to scrape at the pier, and the thuds as the hull struck it could be heard all the way up at the front steps. Anna was trudging along in her black leather jacket, up the gravel path on the slope, past the low bushes that had been planted unmercifully on the lawn. I don't know if they were meant to look like some sort of bower, but if they were, it was an unsuccessful one. This was not a place to thrive in. A cold gust of wind tore at me up on the stairs, and I watched as Anna tottered on the hillside below. I had been studying the weather forecasts for several weeks, trying to determine which days would be optimal, but in the end I had to give up. It was impossible, in these circumstances, to say whether the weather would be on our side or not, as fast as it changed out here.

Once inside the hall, I received the key to my room from the secretary, walked up the stairs, unlocked the door, closed it behind me, and quickly began to unpack. Just as I finished, the secretary yanked the door open without knocking.

"Assembly in ten minutes. Come on down; be your most pleasant self. Don't act suspicious. Don't miss anything."

I wanted to ask him about the true state of Anna's health and tell him that what I had seen so far was worrying, but I didn't have time before he closed the door again.

The round of introductions on the ground floor was really rather dull. I noticed that the secretary didn't mention my military rank when he introduced me, but I also understood that it was better if the others didn't know. Don't attract unnecessary attention; don't appear to be a threat or a competitor. The only thing of note, aside from the fact that Lotte Colliander became upset when they forgot to introduce her, was how uncomfortable Anna seemed when it was time for her introduction. The secretary was precisely the type of authority Anna usually had issues with, so I assumed she thought he was an imbecile, and I had expected that she would start to challenge him on some detail or another, the way she always used to do when we were colleagues ("Well, technically, we weren't actually *in* Kyzyl Kum, but just outside it, or at least on the border . . ."), but instead she remained silent and seemed to be studying some detail of the carpet pattern, her jaw set, as the secretary went on about her merits. When the meeting was over and the room emptied of people, she stayed behind, standing near the window. Her shoulders looked more angular and narrow than ever, and I felt the urge to wrap her in a blanket. But instead I went over and tried to initiate a conversation as naturally as possible, both to guarantee that she wouldn't give either me or herself away to the others, and also to try to figure out how much she had guessed. It went well at first, but suddenly, as we were talking, she smiled that smile again. She excused herself rather suddenly, and I ended up standing there watching her thin figure vanish up the stairs.

When she was out of sight, I went the same way, only to my own room, and stretched out on the bed. I knew why I had accepted the assignment. It was the right decision, perfectly reasonable, and the thought of that made me feel a touch calmer, but I still couldn't help wishing there was another way out of this.

ANNA

I DIDN'T NOTICE it had gotten dark out until I walked down the grand staircase to join the others. I wondered if Henry was still in his room, and for a brief moment I considered knocking on his door to see if he wanted to come down with me, but then I decided against it, so as not to risk being rebuffed. It was as if anything to do with him was really taxing for me. I went down the grand staircase and stopped on a landing halfway down, where large floor-to-ceiling windows looked out at the sea. The house bore the same touches as all the party's official buildings. Photographs of great leaders on the walls; pastel-colored, national romantic-style paintings that all party members seemed to love—waterfalls and forests, blond children playing around farm equipment, moose peering out of the woods near hydroelectric plants. All the floors were covered in the obligatory linoleum. But there were also a few details that hinted that this house had once seen a different time, the same time that appeared to rule down on the Strategic Level. An old escritoire, an upholstered velvet chair with brass fittings. Dark wood; heavy, scrolled carvings. Objects that had been made by hand rather than produced in factories. I wondered how old this building really was. It must have been here long before we entered the Union, part of the old world, Nour's world. The staircase I was standing on looked as if it had been salvaged from the *Titanic*, and when I ran my hand along the shiny black wood of the banister it made me feel a little more secure, as if Nour were watching over me. This feeling surprised me, since Nour had never been much of a mother hen. More like a mother dinosaur, the type who laid her egg and then walked away. I wondered what she and Siri were doing right then. Maybe they were eating dinner; maybe they were watching TV; maybe Siri was already under the blanket with the blue bubbles, looking up at the ceiling and wondering what I was doing. Maybe she didn't think about me at all. I found myself gazing out the window into the darkness, as if there were a chance I could see what they were up to, before I realized that the window looked the other direction, away from land, out to sea. I leaned even closer to the window to find out if I could see anything in the darkness. My breath made a frosty circle on the pane; apparently it was cold out, and the chill from the window sent tiny, prickling contractions through my whole body. I could hear the rumbling sound of strong winds causing the windowpanes to sing a dull, cavelike song. Through the great windows I could see the moon suspended above the horizon, huge and yellow like in a drawing, shining a lovely moon-path on the sea. There was nothing out there but sea. Shiny, cold, wet, dark, deep. No other islands, no boats, nothing. Suddenly something came rushing toward the window and struck it right in front of my face. I screeched and jumped backward, tripping over my own feet, feeling my heels roll on the step behind me. I was about to fall down the stairs. My hands snatched at the railing, and I caught it. The adrenaline that had instantly been pumped out into my body began to abate just as rapidly once I realized that it must have been a branch whipping the pane just in front of my face. From a tree, probably; it was too dark to tell. I looked back at the window, but by now I was too far away to make out any details in the darkness outside. The interior lighting turned the window into a mirror, and all I could see was my own frightened face floating in the uneven, handblown glass panes. I put my hands to my cheeks as if to calm the panicky adrenaline that was still washing through my body, and when it felt like I had everything back under control I continued downstairs.

DINNER PREPARATIONS WERE in full swing when I stepped into the spacious kitchen. I looked around and almost wanted to rub my eyes. I had never seen such overabundance. The counters were heaped with food: meats, pâtés, pierogi, aspics—all sorted by date and labeled with instructions. The evening's dinner appeared to consist of entrées the others were just putting into the oven on large baking sheets. I noticed the familiar seal of the parliamentary restaurant on the trays. Apparently they'd been the ones in charge of catering. I wondered if this extravagance was meant to maintain some sort of expected standard for the more prominent candidates. Both Jon and Franziska found it perfectly normal to eat lunches and dinners at restaurants that ordinary citizens didn't even have access to.

I had never been there myself, of course, and if I ever had been I'm sure I wouldn't have been able to enjoy the food because I would have been spending all my energy on feeling out of place: observed and unseen all at once. On the table was a large basket of fresh fruit: bananas, pineapples, papayas, grapes, passion fruit, and coconuts. I realized as I stared at a coconut that I had no idea what it actually tasted like.

The others were already hard at work, moving food in and out of fridges and ovens, chatting all the while. I remained standing in the doorway, and just as it had many times before, it felt like there was a thin film of plastic between me and everyone else. They seemed so comfortable in their bodies, so relaxed, so incredibly natural in their human costumes. I always found it a strain to spend time with other people, and I was deeply envious of them, of this thing they apparently weren't even aware they were doing: the ease with which they were together. *But what do I know?* I thought. *What do I know about the costs of this?* Maybe they were like gymnasts, who always seem to twist effortlessly into somersaults in the air, when in fact they have tens of thousands of hours of pain, practice, tears, and hopelessness behind them. Maybe it was like that. But I was still envious of them.

"Red or white?"

I twisted around to look over my shoulder. Beside me stood the colonel with his arms full of wine bottles that looked like props from a pirate play. Some of them were even dusty.

"What a fantastic wine cellar they have here! Truly well stocked. There's everything imaginable, even French and Italian wines! I checked with the Chairman and he said that it's just fine to go browse through it."

He held up one bottle and looked at it with the sort of loving gaze most men reserve for their wives, or possibly their cars.

"Dear God, Bordeaux wines . . . it's been ages," he mumbled, almost to himself. Then he looked at me with those brilliant blue eyes that made him look like a little boy.

"Just between us, no offense to Black Sea wines, but this . . . this is something else, let me tell you. May I tempt you with a dry Sancerre . . . or maybe something stronger?"

"I have no idea what you're talking about. Red is fine," I said.

"Aha! Good, good. And do you have any preferences? Light? Fruity? Dry?"

"No, you choose. You seem like the right man for the job."

The colonel smiled contentedly, turned on his heel, and slipped back into the bustle of the kitchen. I thought he seemed kind. It was an uncomfortable thought, given what I was about to subject him to.

The colonel returned with two ridiculously large wineglasses in hand and held one out to me. Although it looked like there was just a splash of wine in the bottom, I suspected he had poured half a bottle into it.

"See if you like this!"

I accepted the glass and took a sip. The flavors blossomed one after the next: fruits, something woody, something dull, something bright. It was the most fantastic wine I had ever tasted. I stared at him in wonder and he nodded delightedly.

"Thought as much. So. Kyzyl Kum?"

I automatically looked away, as I always did when it came up. The colonel seemed to be an observant person, someone who had spent his entire professional life training himself to read people and evaluate what they said (and didn't say). I tried to appear as nonchalant as possible.

"Yep."

The colonel swirled the wine in his glass for a moment, then went on in the same low tone, just loud enough for me to hear what he was saying, just quiet enough so that no one else would overhear any of our conversation.

"I hope you don't mind my asking. I'm genuinely interested. I was stationed near there myself, before the turn of the century."

I knew this already, from back when I was working with the personal dossiers, that the colonel and I had this in common, even though I hadn't been prepared for him to bring it up so directly.

"I understand if it's not something you want to or even maybe can discuss. That sort of thing can be very difficult to talk about. Very few people understand it."

His tone conveyed neither judgment nor blame; instead it was quite friendly. The two of us watched the others in the kitchen. I saw Henry slicing vegetables on the other side of the kitchen table, engrossed in what appeared to be a somewhat captivating conversation with Lotte, while Franziska took a baking sheet from the large, shiny convection oven, and I inwardly thanked myself for sparing myself that knock on Henry's door and the feeling of foolishness when it didn't open. I probably would have read far too much into it.

"Thanks," I said simply to the colonel. It felt like I should say something more, but I couldn't think of what and so just stood there silently beside him, holding my wineglass. The silence wasn't uncomfortable; instead it felt restful. Under different circumstances, he might have been a person I really could have talked to.

"How did you happen to end up here?" I asked him. Even if I wasn't as clever at it as Henry was, I still understood his basic principle—start talking about the other person instead of changing the subject. People love talking about themselves, almost everyone does.

The colonel looked at me with one eyebrow raised in amusement.

"Perhaps you think that I look a little too old for this type of assignment? That I should be retired, sitting on Rügen and nursing my arthritis? Well, you might be right. But you know, it's hard for someone who has spent his whole life giving and obeying orders to refuse when someone tells you to *go*. And I do still work. Not the way I used to, certainly, but I'm still in the service. Behind a desk. Throughout the years I have discovered that you can accomplish things there as well, isn't that right?"

"Where are you stationed now?"

"On staff. Unfortunately, that's all I can tell you."

"I understand," I said, mostly to have something to say.

"Do you?" He still looked amused, as if he didn't quite believe me. "It does seem a little silly these days, all this secrecy. Sure, there are some instances when it's justified, but for the most part it's just a way for people to make themselves feel special and interesting. Or maybe you disagree?" the colonel went on. "Maybe you're the sort who wants to stamp 'classified' on everything?"

"Is this one of those instances?" I asked him.

"One of what?"

"One of the instances where secrecy is justified."

The colonel stood there for a moment without responding, stroking his chin thoughtfully.

"Yes," he said at last. "Yes, this time I think it really is justified."

BEFORE I COULD formulate my next question, Lotte Colliander approached us and held out a stack of plates. I handed my wineglass to the colonel so I could take them.

"Would you mind setting the table?"

Without waiting for a response, she piled a bunch of linen napkins on top of the plates. I was balancing an unsteady tower in my hands.

"Where are we eating?"

"In the parlor. They're in the process of setting up tables in there right now."

I looked around the kitchen again. Jon von Post and Katja were missing. I wondered if Katja was already in the parlor because she was preparing for the next step in our assignment. If so, perhaps I had underestimated her a bit. I followed Lotte. Her stride was efficient; she was dressed in a navy blue pencil skirt and practical kitten heels. Not too high, not too low. Although she was quite short and presumably only a year or two older than me, I felt like I was fetching books for the teacher. She was the type of person who seemed to have been born an adult. She bobbed her head slightly, as if she had heard my thoughts and was dismissing them.

＃ ＃ ＃

I HEARD JON von Post's voice even before we entered the parlor.

". . . so then I told him there was no chance that would get approval. But he's stubborn. Of course he wouldn't listen, even though . . ."

Lotte knocked at the door as she opened it, but then we just stood there. Jon and Katja were on the other side of the room, Katja with her back to the wall and Jon leaning over her with his hand against the wall, blocking any escape. He was standing just barely too close, so you wouldn't have noticed it if it weren't for Katja's pained expression and how relieved she was to see us step in.

"Great, there are the plates!"

Jon looked nowhere near as uncomfortable as Katja did. In fact, he looked pleased. Clearly he had no problem standing way too close to a woman who didn't want him to. No new story there.

I couldn't see Lotte's face, but she straightened her back and let slip a heavy sigh, as if this were something she had seen far too many times. And I'm sure she had, too. Conference centers, dinners, liquor tables. Increasingly drunk men with their thick wallets and their privilege, pouring glass after glass of vodka, becoming more and more erratic and indiscreet, feeling a growing urge to have and take, ever more inclined to place the blame on both those who said yes and those who said no. She was asking for it. Fucking prudish whore. Despite all the equality projects and state policy documents about fair treatment, it was still always the same thing.

"We certainly don't mean to interrupt, but we're here to set the table."

Lotte strode confidently to the table, grabbed a tablecloth that was folded on top of the lovely, glossy jacaranda surface, and began to shake it out. Katja seized the opportunity, wriggled past Jon, took the other end of the tablecloth, and helped Lotte draw it evenly across the table. I entered the room and, with a certain amount of effort, set my wobbly stack of plates on a small serving table. Jon remained near the wall, bouncing on his heels with a glass in his hand. Apparently it didn't even occur to him to help.

Katja cast a quick glance at me to see if I was on the same page, and then she said loudly, "Does anyone know where the wineglasses are? I could find only the little port glasses in here."

Lotte, who seemed to be the sort of person who was almost pathologically compelled to take command of every situation, took the bait at once:

"I know where they are. They're in the kitchen; let's go get them. Come on, you can help me carry them."

She gave Jon a commanding look, and at last he seemed to catch on that she expected him to lend a hand. I took a few steps after them and closed the door to the dining room as quietly as I could once they had left. I turned to Katja.

"Do you have the glasses?" she whispered. "I have the stuff here. You'll have to do it." She handed me the little tube.

THE SECRETARY TOOK out a transparent vial with a tiny dropper at the top and gave it to me. In the yellow light of the Strategic Level, the liquid looked yellow as well.

"This is a sedative. It is tasteless and colorless, and it takes only one drop to cause drowsiness. It has the advantage of several hours' delay before the substance begins to take full effect."

He looked at Katja as if to confirm that he had understood the medical effects correctly, and then he turned to me again.

"So it's best to make sure to keep good track of your own glasses."

"We'll put it into the port glasses," Katja explained. *"Once people have had a couple of glasses with dinner they won't pay much attention to whether everyone else is drinking or not."*

"Good," said the secretary, *"so all you have to do is get one drop in each glass without anyone noticing. It won't knock them out completely, of course, nor do we want it to, because that would seem suspicious, but it will make things a little easier when it's time for you to . . . well, to do what you have to do. And don't forget—two drops in the primary witness's glass."*

WHEN ONLY THE colonel's glass remained, we heard steps and approaching voices.

"Hurry, hurry!" Katja exclaimed as I dropped in a double dose, carefully, carefully: tiny, tiny drops which wouldn't even be visible on the bottom of the glass. Cool and collected, I plugged the dropper and quickly stuck it through the neckline of my shirt and into my bra. Katja stared at the door. She had seemed so calm and confident earlier, but now she almost seemed to be panicking with stress, and I wondered how much fieldwork she'd actually logged.

"Stop looking so guilty and start setting the table," I hissed through my teeth as I handed her all but two of the place cards, which I put down where I stood and at the spot beside it. Then I went to get the stack of plates from the serving table, and I had just lifted them up when the others came through the door. The colonel and Franziska were first, and Henry was right behind them. He stopped in the doorway for a moment and looked around.

"Do you need help with anything?"

"You can take a few of these," I said, nodding at the plates in my arms.

He walked up to me and lifted away half of the stack.

"Classic Anna Francis, picking up all of them at once," he said quietly, flashing a grin.

"So observant and insightful of you to perform such a fundamental analysis of my personality when you met me for the first time only a few hours ago," I said back, just as quietly.

He smiled again and then said, at a normal volume, "How do you want these on the table?"

"One large and one small one at each place. I'm sure you can handle it."

Henry nodded and began to set out the plates, starting at the end of the table. I did the same, from the other direction. As usual, my eyes were caught by his hands as they handled the plates. There was a precision to his movements, a sort of economy. Not too much and not too little. I looked away and concentrated on my own task.

When I was little, Nour called me Miss Smithereens because I broke glasses and plates so often. Part of Nour's teachings on labor and the worth of money involved cleaning up after yourself if you broke something. Plus a deduction from my weekly allowance. "You have to learn what things cost," she liked to say. But this time, I didn't drop anything. Henry and I walked around each other with the large and small plates and then the napkins, knives, forks, more cutlery, wineglasses (which eventually showed up when Jon and Lotte brought them in) without speaking; it was like silent, harmonious choreography as we moved in relation to one another, around and around the table. The room filled with food and drink, and at last we were ready and everyone was able to take a seat.

It was an unusual group who gathered around the table and began to pass the appetizers. Small hors d'oeuvres, canapés, made of pretty, hard-to-identify ingredients. One reddish salad, one greenish one; some sort of leaf, a cube of smoked meat, a slice of pale fish. It was the appetizer version of the "seven sorts of cookies" tradition. The colonel, whom I had seated next to me, passed each little platter on to me, and I passed them on to Henry, who was sitting across from me. Next to him were first Lotte, then Franziska—and when I looked at her plate, I realized that she had not, of course, taken one of each option but had selected two microscopic pieces, which she was now pushing around the plate. I couldn't blame her. There weren't many older women who managed to stay on TV year after year. Most of them were switched out in favor of younger talent when they were around fifty. Women who made less of a fuss and cost less money. Who were more agreeable. The fact that the Minister of the Interior was her brother-in-law surely must have made things easier for Franziska; in fact, I'd already heard her go into great detail about it. Contacts equaled power, and if you had them you could afford to make demands. But apparently not gain weight.

Franziska noticed that I was looking at her plate, and her eyes moved to my own overfull one.

"My, aren't you hungry!"

You could have shredded paper in the corners of her mouth, her smile was so cutting. I wanted to say something back, scrutinize her, let her know that I knew she was trying to bully me, but I quickly realized that it wasn't worth fighting. I would be spending only one night with her. So instead I looked down at my food and hmm'd noncommittally. But it bothered me that she was going to walk around thinking she'd shut me up and shamed me.

THE SECRETARY TURNED *to look at me.*

"Your task is to drink the witness under the table."

I looked back at the secretary and awaited the explanation.

"The witness, that is, the person Katja will wake up once you're dead. The one who will confirm that you have died. Make sure to sit next to him at dinner. You don't know who it will be yet, but it will be the person who is assigned the room on the ground floor."

The secretary pointed at the floor plan that was spread out on the table.

"We'll block off some of the rooms on the second floor, blame it on water damage, so that one person will have to sleep on the ground floor, which will make it logical for him to be the one the doctor wakes when she 'finds' you."

"And my job is to drink him under the table during dinner."

"Yes; after all, we don't want him to be too observant when he has to view and move a living corpse."

"So we're going to drug him and get him drunk?"

The secretary pursed his lips at my disapproving tone.

"Well, in these sorts of situations it's better safe than sorry. The effect of the drug will increase the more he drinks, and the groggier he is when he is woken up, the better. Plus, it shouldn't be very hard to do. He's an alcoholic."

"WOULD YOU LIKE more wine?"

I didn't wait for an answer, just took the bottle and refilled the colonel's glass.

"Thank you, thank you!"

He immediately lifted the glass to his mouth and took a large gulp. I quickly glanced around at everyone else's glasses; sure enough, the colonel had drained his long before the others. Most people finish their first three glasses as a group; they drink at about the same speed as the people they're drinking with. After a few glasses, once the buzz has shaved off the first layer of self-consciousness and control, that effect tapers off. It's unusual for people to do what the colonel was doing and drink faster than the rest of their company right from the start. Unless they have a drinking problem, that is.

IT WAS A strange, tentative conversation going on at the table. All the participants were unique, interesting, competent, used to being the life of the party. What's more, they were all in competition for the same job. And even if I didn't know what sort of position they were preparing for, it was apparently so desirable that everyone present thought it was worth spending a few days on a godforsaken island in the outer archipelago. It also seemed, thus far, that everyone was obeying the Chairman and not discussing their assignment with anyone else. I assumed they didn't want to destroy their own chances by gossiping. Jon and Franziska had found some sort of conversational method in which they took turns talking about themselves as soon as the other stopped to take a breath. The conversation was muddled, since neither was actually listening to what the other said. I heard them refer endlessly to various celebrities in politics and business by first name. An invisible canon of Very Important People they were apparently attempting to impress one another with. Katja was sitting on the end of the table between them, listening. The few times she tried to break into the conversation and get a word in, she was quickly pushed back out.

AT OUR END of the table, Henry was the one who had invisibly taken command, and he had done so in his usual manner, by getting others to talk. From the way he alternately asked questions of the colonel and refilled his wineglass, I suspected that he had also become aware of the colonel's weak spot and was trying to exploit it, just as I was. On the one hand, this was a good thing, because it meant I could sit back and let him do the work; on the other hand, I wondered what reason Henry had to try to booze the colonel under the table. Maybe it was his competitive nature; maybe he wanted to increase his own chances of getting the job by putting the colonel out of play or at least casting him in a bad light. Lotte broke into the conversation now and then, and as her shoulders sagged lower and lower she became less boastfully self-involved and more interested in the rest of us. Suddenly she turned directly to me.

"So what do you do now that you're back home?"

I hesitated in responding.

"I've gone back to my usual job."

Lotte looked surprised.

"That's unexpected. I thought you would have been given some top job, after all the buzz surrounding you."

I didn't know whether she noticed my reaction, because she continued in a friendlier manner, as if to take the edge off her snide tone.

"It seems like you did a fantastic job. Difficult. It must be incredibly demanding to work in a place like that."

I hmm'd noncommittally a little and kept chewing my food, which seemed to expand in my mouth.

"At least it's lucky that you don't have a family to worry about. My husband and children would never let me go off to a place like that."

"I have a daughter," I said before I could stop myself, and I immediately regretted it.

Lotte looked surprised.

"Oh, how old is she?"

"Nine."

"Well . . . I see. Okay. Was she with you? No, she couldn't have been, right?"

"She lived with my mother while I was gone."

Lotte appeared to be waiting for me to say something

more. My brain was rushing around looking for things I could say that wouldn't invite any more painful explanation.

"How many kids do you have?"

Henry had come to my rescue. I wondered if he had seen the panic in my eyes. Lotte turned to him.

"Well, they're older now, and they don't need my full attention all the time, so that's why I am able to consider this position in the first place, but they're twelve and fourteen—boys. One . . ."

She babbled on about hockey practice and the quality of various schools. I didn't dare to look at Henry; I just kept focusing on Lotte, and eventually I managed to squeeze out a question or two that made her keep talking about herself, and the conversation slowly moved to safer ground.

WHEN I TOLD Nour I was pregnant, I made sure to put it off until it was too late to have an abortion. Probably because I knew that was what she would suggest, and I was right. We were sitting in her kitchen, it was a Sunday, and Nour had seemed surprised when I told her I wanted to come visit her, but she hadn't asked why, just told me I was welcome. When I got there, she had gone so far as to put coffee on the kitchen table, and some sort of dry buns, which had probably been in her cupboard for months. I wondered who had brought them over; as far as I was aware, Nour didn't get many visitors anymore. It seemed unlikely that she had bought them herself, much less baked them.

In my mind, I had thought up the perfect sentence, a sentence that would convey all the information and answer all her questions in one elegant formulation, while simultane-ously closing all the doors on any solution but the one I had already chosen. "I found out I'm pregnant and since it's too late for an abortion I'm going to keep the baby." It should have worked, but it didn't, because Nour didn't say anything. Then she took out her ever-present pack of little brown cigarillos, reached for the matches on the table, puffed until it was lit, took a deep drag, blew it out, and looked thoughtfully at the smoke.

"Seriously, you're going to smoke right now?"

"This is my kitchen, and you're here of your own free will," Nour said, standing up to get an ashtray.

She came back, sat down, and continued to look at me.

"How many weeks are you?"

"Nineteen. So as you know, it's too late to get rid of it."

"What if I said it isn't too late?"

"What do you mean?"

I felt myself break into a cold sweat. The scent of the coffee mixed with the smell of the smoke in the air, and nausea rose in my throat.

"I might know someone who can fix it anyway. You used to be able to get an abortion until the twenty-second week, you know, if there were extenuating circumstances. Rape or illness or insanity. If the mother was considered unfit. That kind of thing."

The nausea was getting stronger; there was a sour taste in my mouth and my pulse was pounding in my ears.

"So that's what you think? I'm an unfit mother and I ought to get rid of it?"

"I'm just saying that it's not easy to be a single mother."

Nour's tone was hard and curt. She leaned across the table.

"Do you really want this child, Anna? Do you want to be like me? Do you want to be on your own with a kid who will keep you from working, keep you from . . ."

She suddenly stopped talking. My cheeks went hot. It was like she had slapped me. I stood up on awkward feet and swayed a little. It wasn't quite the sort of decisive movement I had intended. Nour refused to meet my gaze, looking stubbornly out the window instead.

"I'm just saying it's not that easy," she said at last.

"Nour, I'm terribly sorry for destroying your exciting life and your career by being born, and I apologize from the bottom of my heart . . ." My voice was on its way up to an unpleasant falsetto, and I could hear how ridiculous I sounded, but I didn't care. "But this child is mine, and I'm not going to get rid of it and I will take care of it and love it and just because it was apparently so fucking hard for you doesn't mean it will be hard for me. I'm going to keep it, and you just have to accept that."

She continued to gaze out the window, pursing her lips slightly in annoyance, and then she said in a caustic voice, "Well, then I suppose I'll just have to say congratulations and good luck. See you when you come crashing down. Because you will. Make no mistake."

I yanked my cardigan from the back of the chair where I had been sitting, my head spinning, but before I left I bent over the table.

"Do you know what the fucking ironic part is, Nour? It's that *you're* giving me advice about parenting. If I were you I would keep my mouth shut about that."

I walked into the hall, my head held high, then bent to tie my shoes with hands that were shaking with rage. It was already more difficult for me to reach my feet easily, even though I wasn't showing very much yet. Then I put on my jacket and walked through the door and down the stairs. I knew I would spend the next few days, weeks, months, playing this conversation backward and forward in my head, that I would regret every word a thousand times over, that I would want to take them back; I would curse myself for not saying something totally different, or for saying anything at all, but at the moment I was full of adrenaline and self-righteous anger that caused my feet to fly over the street. It felt like liberation.

I didn't see Nour again during my entire pregnancy. Not until after Siri was born and she showed up at the hospital with that confection of a dress and a new chapter began.

FOOD WAS BROUGHT and taken away, more bottles were uncorked and passed around. Cheese and dessert. More wine. The company had broken into smaller groups. Franziska had traded places with Katja, and now she and Jon were engrossed in a conversation that looked more like foreplay. Franziska was laughing with her head thrown back, fingering her collarbone; Jon sat with his legs spread, leaning forward, as if he might dip his face into her décolletage at any moment. Katja had initiated a conversation with Lotte; it seemed to be of interest to them both, something about cross-country skiing. The buzz of conversation grew louder and louder around the table. Most people were starting to become noticeably tipsy, myself included, as I discovered to my own horror. When Katja served the small glasses of port, not a single person declined, nor did anyone notice that neither she nor I was drinking from our glasses. It was around ten o'clock, which placed my impending death five hours in the future.

I found Henry watching me several times during dinner. He didn't look away when I gazed back. And when some of the company began to rise from the table, he suddenly stood up, rounded the table, and placed a hand on my shoulder.

"Can I get you anything? Whiskey, brandy, wine?"

"I'd love a big glass of water."

I wondered if Henry would do what he always used to at those few work parties he had actually attended in previous years—suddenly make a move, thank everyone, and vanish—but he came back with the glass and sat back down across from me. Our fingers brushed when he handed me the glass; I wondered if that was by accident. After a while, I felt his foot against my own. I looked at him; he was listening to the colonel with an attentive expression, pretending not to notice me even as he moved his leg slightly farther between mine, until our knees overlapped. The tablecloth was quite long on the end, where we were sitting, so no one could see what was going on. I gently squeezed my knees around his; he pressed back.

So that was that. It wasn't just in my head, everything that had happened within me. It was in him too. It was both a relief and a sorrow. The timing could hardly have been worse. When the colonel eased his grip on the conversation, Henry leaned toward me. His eyes were large, his pupils dilated.

"Do you know if there's any way to land a boat on the other side of the island?"

"No idea, why?" I lied.

"Now that the wind has come up it might be good to know if there's anywhere besides the pier where the boat can put in to get us."

I looked at him curiously until I realized what he was getting at.

"Maybe we should go out and check."

Henry looked like this was a brand-new idea for him, and it struck me again how good he was at putting up a front.

"That might be smart. Shall we go for a walk?"

We stood up at the same time.

"Are you off to bed already?"

The colonel looked disappointed. The alcohol, and maybe even the drugs at the bottom of his empty port glass, had begun to seriously affect him. Gone was the attentive person I had met earlier that day; in his place was a self-absorbed old man who droned on and on about his own affairs, his gaze turning ever more inward. The secretary had been right about the colonel's alcoholism—he was draining and refilling his glass more and more swiftly.

"We're just going to check how windy it is; we'll be right back!"

The colonel pushed his chair back and I was afraid he was about to offer to come with us, but Henry cleverly warded him off.

"Maybe you could go explore the wine cellar in the meantime? I hear you know all about vintages and grapes and stuff. Anna told me we have you to thank for the fantastic wine we drank with dinner."

The colonel allowed himself to be flattered and promised

he would do his best to pick out a few exceptional bottles for the table by the time we returned, and before he could elaborate we managed to leave the room.

HENRY HANDED ME my jacket from the rack in the hall. We dressed in silence and opened the large front door. Outside, the wind was stiff. Henry had to lean against the door with his shoulder. He wasn't a large man, but he managed to force it open. We walked beside each other, down to the beach behind the house, in silence. It was as if the gale had interrupted our flirting. Henry walked with his hands thrust deep into the pockets of his coat, and I wondered if he regretted his move, or if he simply hadn't made one; perhaps I had misunderstood or misinterpreted him after all.

We stopped once we reached the shore. Henry looked around.

"No chance you could put in here with this wind," he said after a moment. "Look at those cliffs out that way. And if this keeps up, the boat won't be able to dock on the other side either, even though it's more sheltered there. If it storms, we'll be totally isolated."

I had almost managed to forget the reason we had come out, because I had assumed it was all pretense, but this caught my attention. He turned around to look at me.

"And the storm is coming. Look at the clouds; look how fast they're moving."

Gray clouds were racing across the moon, impossibly fast, as if in an animation. I looked at Henry again. Our faces were close. His gaze was like smoke in a globe of glass. Our eyes locked. I couldn't break away and I couldn't get closer.

"What are you really doing here?" he whispered.

"What do you want with me?" I whispered back.

Suddenly Henry broke the spell.

"Well, maybe it's best to go back," he said curtly, as he turned back toward the house and started walking.

I trudged after him. With every passing second, I felt dumber and dumber, more and more duped, exposed, unmasked. I had lowered my guard, I had shown myself to be weak; my actions were just as stupid and embarrassing as you would expect from an amateur with no experience in top-secret assignments. I had acted like a lovesick teenager, just as awkward as I always feared I would be in Henry's company. I knew this part of my tipsy self, a part of me that could get hung up on an injustice, a wording, an offense, and then ruminate on it for hours—and I hated it. I felt the lump in my stomach grow and the tears spring into my eyes. Just as I was about to open my mouth to say something to Henry, he tugged at my arm and roughly dragged me around the edge of a cliff. He put his hand over my mouth, gently, and whispered "shh" and pointed at Lotte, who was coming down the steep path. She stopped and stood there just around the corner of the house, quite close to where we were, and to my great surprise she opened her purse and took out a large, ungainly satellite phone, which by all appearances was fully functional. She was calling someone, and I heard her greet the person on the other end. I concentrated on trying to hear what she was saying, but she was too far away and the wind carried off her words.

Henry was standing close behind me. I felt his breath against the exposed portion of my neck, between my coat and my hairline. He pressed his body to mine, his lips brushing just behind my ear. It felt like sticking a key in a lock and turning it, and when I placed his arm around my waist I realized I didn't care about all the rest. The assignment, who he truly was, how it would end. Or anything but this.

Some small part of my consciousness heard Lotte bring the conversation to a close and vanish back up to the house. I remained in Henry's arms, as still as if I had spotted a deer.

"Come on," he said. "We can't stay here."

HIS BODY WAS slighter than I thought, thinner. His face was slightly round, and that was probably why I expected him to have the typical middle-aged male office body, with extra layers of fat as insolation, soft bulges on either side of his spine, and a protruding belly. But as my hands and eyes searched their way forward in the bluish darkness of his room, I realized that he was much closer to gaunt. His chest was flat and his collarbones cast shadows on the skin below; I let my fingers follow them toward his midline and down his sternum. His body, which had been so impossible to imagine, became almost repellently real under my hands. To see him at such close range, every hair, every angle, was like the beam of a flashlight straight into my eyes, so I closed them and let my hands go before my gaze. His hands were moving over me as well, as if he were reading Braille, registering the line that was the lower edge of my shoulder blade, the vertical protrusions of my spine, the hard roundness of my hip bones. When I was little, I had a "magic coloring book," a book with clean white pages, but when you dragged a wet paintbrush over them, shapes and colors and flowers appeared. That was how it felt when Henry moved his hands on my body, as if each part of me he touched came to life in tiny bubbles of carbonation.

I didn't cry out when I came, and neither did he, because this wasn't the sort of sex you had to exaggerate. And it wasn't the best sex I ever had, but it wasn't far from it.

AFTERWARD, AS WE lay on our backs next to each other on the bed, he distractedly ran the back of his index finger across my cheek. His room was dark, but the curtains in the window were open, and the clouds were still rushing past the moon, untiring in the night sky.

"What are you thinking about, Anna?" he murmured, almost to himself.

"Betrayal," I said. He sleepily turned his face to me.

"What did you say?"

"Betrayal. I know how it feels."

I turned my face to the ceiling and studied the thin cracks in the paint; they stood out in the pale moonlight like blood vessels. My thoughts welled up, fast and overwhelming. If I allowed myself to think about it, even the tiniest bit, I would still be able to taste the iron on my tongue, the flavor of betrayal, of being betrayed, of failure, of making the wrong decision. I couldn't let myself think like that, I knew it was bad for me. But my thoughts drifted off of their own accord, and suddenly I was back in the cold tent camp. I was gripped by the sudden longing to tell him everything, everything about Kyzyl Kum and what really happened there at the end, everything about this assignment, everything about the betrayal I

was about to commit, about the betrayal I had, in some ways, already committed.

Henry stroked my cheek with the back of his finger again.

"Try to get some sleep," he said, and then he kissed me on the cheek, turned over so his back was to me, pulled the blanket over his head, and grew still. I lay there staring at the ceiling, listening to his breaths become long, even, deep. There was a faint rattle every time he inhaled, so I stayed a little bit longer, just so I could be close to him for one last stolen moment. Then I stood up, put on my clothes, sneaked through the dark room on bare feet, slowly pressed the door handle down, opened the door a crack, and cautiously slipped out to be murdered.

WHEN I ARRIVED in the kitchen, Katja was already there. She was pacing back and forth in annoyance.

"Close the door behind you and lock it. I thought you would never show up!"

Katja kneeled on the floor. She was dressed in some sort of exercise outfit, and as she dove into her bag I noticed the logo of the Leningrad ballet on her back. That explained her good posture, but I assumed she must have been pretty young when she quit, before she had time to get injured and worn out, because she appeared to move with no pain or stiffness in her body even now, in the middle of the night.

"When did you quit dancing?" I asked, mostly to have something to say.

"Are you really going to make small talk right now?" Katja hissed quietly.

I sat down on the floor beside her and shut up while she removed one thing after the next from her bag. Syringes, cannulas, small glass bottles with labels, compresses—she arranged it all in straight, even lines on a small towel I assumed was hospital green, but it was hard to determine the color in the dark. I looked at the instruments and shuddered.

"Lie down on your back," Katja whispered, and I did as she said.

And then it began. Katja picked up a strange ink pad. She donned a pair of vinyl gloves and pressed her fingers against the pad one by one. Then she grabbed my throat and squeezed gently, letting her fingernails dig in a little deeper.

"Move your head a little, or else this won't leave believable bruises."

I did as she said and she held on with gentle but determined hands. When she was done, she took out a little flashlight and shone it on my throat, then nodded, satisfied.

"Looks good," she said.

I was about to thank her out of sheer reflex, but I stopped myself. Instead I lay there in silence as Katja tinkered with different syringes next to me. She bent over me.

"I'm going to give you an injection in the top of your tongue now, so it looks like you've been strangled in case anyone looks in your mouth. Your airways will remain open, so you can still breathe."

I nodded.

"Ready?" Katja asked, and without waiting for my agreement she grabbed my head firmly. "Open wide and stick out your tongue."

I did as she said. But just as she was about to stick me, I realized this was my last chance to say something.

"Katja?"

"Yes?" She looked at me, irritated.

"Are you sure this is going to work?"

"Of course. I'm a doctor, you can trust me."

She bent over again to stick me, but I raised my hand and placed it on her arm.

"Tell me I will wake up again."

She sighed, but I stood my ground.

"You tell me to trust you, and I do, but you're not the one doing this—I am. So I want you, as trustworthy as you say you are, to promise me I will wake up again."

I stared at her; it was hard to read her eyes in the darkness, because when she leaned across me all I could see were two black holes where her eyes were. She didn't say anything for a moment, but then she spoke.

"I promise you'll wake up again. You have my word, on my honor as a doctor."

"Good."

I laid my head back down.

"Can you open up now, please?"

I opened my mouth, stuck out my tongue, and felt the sting. My tongue started swelling right away. I felt panic rise in my head.

"Relax, just breathe through your nose. There you go, long, deep breaths through your nose. Think about babies; they always breathe through their noses when they sleep. There. Good."

I caught my breath and felt the panic sink back down.

"Now I'm going to put drops in your eyes to paralyze your pupils. There will also be tiny bleeds in the whites of your eyes. They'll go away. I'm going to open your eyelids now . . . good. Keep your eyes closed and it won't feel as strange."

I did as she said, and she kept talking. The irritation had vanished from her voice; she was speaking in a calm doctor voice now.

"Now, Anna, I'm going to give you the last injection. This is a sedative and muscle relaxant. It will bring your breathing down to a minimum and your body will go limp. In just a second it will feel like you're falling asleep. It's possible that you will see or hear something while you're out, but it won't be coherent and you won't be able to communicate. Once you're asleep, I'm going to wait until I'm totally sure you're out and then I will run over and pound on the colonel's door just as we agreed. He'll follow me down here, and hopefully he'll be so drunk and drugged that he agrees that you're dead, and we'll carry you down to the chest freezer, where I'll wake you up with an injection as soon as I can. It's going to be uncomfortable, Anna, but you can handle it. Then I'll wake the others, and . . ." Her voice faded as if she were walking backward through a marble hall.

"Count backward, Anna." I heard her voice from the other side of the marble hall, and I started counting silently to myself, one number for each breath. *Ten, nine, eight* the floor felt cold and sticky underneath me *seven, six, five* I thought about Siri in her bed surrounded by the staring stuffed animals with their button eyes it smelled like snow or maybe tasted *four, three* skinny arm soft cheek with sleep hair stuck brush it away with index finger *two, one* good-bye.

✳ ✳ ✳

IT WAS LIKE waking to an elephant sitting on my chest. The pain was sudden and indescribable. I couldn't tell if it was a contraction or an expansion in my rib cage, just that it was horribly painful. I tried to take a breath, with very little success. I tried in vain to focus on the face that was dancing before me, and after a few seconds I realized that it must be Katja's pale face and blond hair I was looking at.

"Anna! Anna! Can you hear me?"

I tried to respond, but the sound that left my mouth was unidentifiable. There was something in my mouth. I turned my head and tried to spit, until I realized it was my own tongue I was trying to spit out. Saliva ran down my cheek. But Katja still seemed satisfied.

"Good. You're coming back. I've given you an injection. Take it easy, you're still under the influence of the drugs."

I tried to sit up, but my body didn't quite obey me. Katja took hold of my arm and stuck a needle into it.

"You'll feel better soon," she said, and she switched to shining a small flashlight right into my eyes.

"Your pupils are still a little sluggish, but that's perfectly normal. Do you think you can sit up?"

I tried again, and it went a little better this time. I managed to straighten out my upper body and pull myself into a sitting position. All at once everything was spinning, and I fumbled for something to hold on to. Katja caught me, and the room around me slowed down. I felt her falter a little as I clung to her arms.

"Anna, listen to me. I understand you don't feel very well right now, but we're in a bit of a hurry. I have to seal up the chest freezer, and you have to get down to the Strategic Level before anyone else comes knocking here. The colonel is upstairs waking the others, and we're supposed to meet in the parlor in ten minutes. He's still dead drunk, so he's not moving too fast. Are you able to make it down now?"

I realized that I was not lying on a cot; I was in the chest freezer. Just as this occurred to me, I also felt how cold it was around me. As if reading my mind, Katja took a shiny foil warming blanket from a shelf behind her.

"Take this with you! You have to get down there right now!"

Katja pressed the refrigeration coil on the wall of the freezer and the hatch opened. She looked considerably less sporty and fit than she had when I met her on the dock. Her eyes were swollen and bloodshot.

"How did the colonel take it?" I asked her.

"Not well. Listen, we can talk about this more later."

She looked anxiously over her shoulder, as if she had seen a noise rather than heard it. With effort, I turned onto my stomach and tried to find the ladder below me with trembling legs.

"I'm going to lock this up now, so no one can open it. You can open it from the inside, using the code, but don't do it unless you have to."

I nodded, grabbed the warming blanket, and threw it down the hatch. Just before I vanished, Katja put her hand on mine.

"Good luck."

She closed the lid of the chest freezer and I heard the lock click as she pressed down. I was alone in the darkness.

# # #

I FUMBLED MY way down the ladder. At the bottom I wrapped the warming blanket around myself again and felt for the light switch on the wall behind me. The yellow light made it feel like evening, although it was almost dawn. I approached the refrigerator on shaky legs, found a bottle containing some sort of sports drink, and drank it in large gulps. My lips felt numb; my tongue was still like a clump of cement in my mouth, and a trickle of the artificially sweet beverage ran from the corner of my mouth and down my neck. I wiped it away with my sleeve, up near my shoulder, in a way you do only when you're absolutely certain you're alone.

I walked over to the little sink and splashed cold water on my face until I started to perk up. My tongue was starting to shrink back to its normal size. I put the warming blanket aside, dug through my bag, and found an undershirt to put on. Then I went over to the door that led to the secret world of the house, the territory between the walls, and walked in. Still shivering, I groped my way up the narrow staircase and reached the curtain that signaled I was on my way to the wall of the parlor. I found the molding and then the holes, pulled aside the hatch, and looked into the room.

NOT EVERYONE HAD arrived yet. Katja was standing closest to the peepholes in the wall, her back toward me. I assumed she had chosen that spot so that I could see as much as possible of the others. Jon was sitting on a chair in ridiculous striped flannel pajamas, looking around drowsily. Next to him sat Franziska in an elegant orange robe with ruffles, her hair still in its usual severe bun, and it looked like she had even taken the time to put on some makeup, or else she had never washed yesterday's off. When Jon looked in the other direction, I noticed that she took the opportunity to adjust the fabric at her cleavage. Lotte was sitting beside Jon in a terry-cloth robe with thick socks on her feet, absentmindedly rubbing her bangs until her hair stood straight up. Next to Lotte was the colonel, in sweatpants and a fleece jacket, red eyed. And then Henry entered the room. I gasped. Just a few hours before, he had been lying naked beside me, and now my hand automatically went to my lips. He cast an indecisive look around the room, then sat down on a chair and aimed an attentive gaze at the door. I got the impression that he was waiting for someone, likely me. Franziska immediately began to complain about why she had been forced to get out of bed, her voice loud so everyone would hear. Katja cut her off and took the floor.

"Thank you for being here, all of you. I'm sorry for rousting you all out of bed in the middle of the night, but the fact is . . . something has happened."

"Shouldn't we wait for Anna?"

This was Henry, interrupting her. He looked around the room again, as if I were there somewhere and he had only missed me. Katja turned to him.

"That's just it. I don't quite know how to say this, but . . ." She took a deep breath and went on.

"Anna is dead."

Although I was completely prepared for her to say something along those lines, a shudder still traveled through my body. *Anna is dead*. If I were to die for real, here and now, no one would have any reason to come looking for me. As far as these people were concerned, I was dead now. It felt creepier than I had expected. I tried to concentrate on what was happening in the room instead of dwelling on that thought. Everyone was staring at Katja as if they didn't understand what she was saying. They looked like overgrown children, with their bewildered faces and nightclothes.

"And unfortunately, I must also inform you that it seems someone has killed her."

I tried to let my eyes move from person to person and make note, in my mind, of their reactions. Jon just stared at Katja with his mouth agape, as if she were speaking an incomprehensible language. Beside him, Franziska looked as if she were frantically searching through her mind for the right question but coming up empty-handed. Lotte looked around the room nervously as she distractedly pulled at her thumbnail like she wanted it to come off, and the colonel hung his head heavily. He was, of course, the only one who wasn't surprised. Just a little while before, he had carried my body to the chest freezer in the medical station. I wondered what his face had looked like then.

But of course, most interesting of all was Henry's reaction. Not just because it was him, but because it was different from the others'. He shrank down as if he had been shot in the back, and now he was bending forward wearily and breathing so hard that his shoulders heaved. Katja tried to give a brief account of what had happened, how she had found me in the kitchen when she got up to get a glass of milk, how she had woken the colonel and how they took me to the chest freezer and locked my body up inside it. Henry stood up suddenly and

walked over to Katja; he said something to her in a low voice.
I couldn't hear what it was, but when she responded I knew
that he had asked to see me. Katja addressed the whole room:

"I'm afraid that's not possible. I have already been in contact with the secretary, who has given me very clear instructions. The body is in a sealed freezer down in the medical
station and no one may open the freezer or touch the body
before we have called in personnel who are able to follow procedure for this type of case."

Only then did the rest of the room appear to grasp what
they had just heard, and a muddle of questions and specula-
tions broke out. Everyone was talking over one another, and
it was hard for me to keep up. Franziska had finally found her
footing and was peppering Katja with one question after the
next: What had happened? *How* had it happened? Was she sure
it wasn't an accident? Was Katja truly qualified to determine
such things? And when would the rescuers arrive? She had
absolutely no intention of remaining on an island where this
sort of thing happened, and she demanded to be allowed to
call the Chairman personally and right away.

"I'm afraid that's not possible either," Katja said again, mechanically, and I wondered how many times she would have
to say this before the stay was over. "The communication radio in the basement appears to be out of order."

"What did you just say?" This was the first time the colonel
had opened his mouth.

"The first time I contacted the secretary it worked just fine,
but the call got cut off, and when I tried to call again it didn't
work. It could be because of the weather."

This was new to me too, and I wondered how it had

happened. Was it really true that the storm had knocked out communications, or was Katja lying so that Franziska wouldn't run off and call the Chairman? I tried to convince myself that it was the latter, but I couldn't help but think that it seemed like a bad omen. Apparently the colonel felt the same, because he suddenly appeared more sober than he had before.

"That's not good," he said succinctly.

"Couldn't she have killed herself?" Lotte suddenly said to no one in particular. When she noticed that everyone's eyes were on her, she went on, her hands tugging and scratching at each other anxiously in her lap. "I mean, I don't know Anna, but from the little I've seen, well . . . she seemed pretty strange, unhappy. Maybe she experienced some sort of trauma while she was gone, and then she came here and . . ."

Lotte's voice grew increasingly louder and faster, as if she were trying to convince herself.

"She told me she had left her child behind and went down there and was part of that war for extended periods, and when I asked her about it she just stopped talking and looked devastated and . . ."

"No, she didn't kill herself," Katja interrupted.

"How do you know? Depression is common in people who have experienced that sort of thing. It has a name . . . post-traumatic stress? Maybe she . . ."

"You can't strangle yourself," Katja said bluntly.

"But . . ."

Lotte deflated a bit and said nothing more.

"She wasn't the type," Henry said, almost to himself, but no one responded; everyone in the room was silent, except for

Lotte, who began to sob quietly and wiped away a few tears with the sleeve of her robe. As I stood there in the dark, cramped space, watching the others, I felt my legs going numb beneath me and a cold sweat begin to trickle down my forehead.

"Could there be someone else on the island?"

This was Jon. He looked at Katja and then, I noticed, at the colonel. Apparently those were the two he expected a sensible answer from. The colonel appeared to consider the question before responding.

"It's a possibility, of course. We'll have to search the island as soon as we can, but before then we should probably try to figure out what happened last night. Who was the last to see Anna?"

I turned my focus to Henry. Since he'd walked up to Katja and demanded to see me, he had collapsed back into his chair and just sat there, head hanging. But now he responded, still without raising his eyes.

"It was probably me." And then something inaudible.

"What?" said the colonel.

"I said, I was sleeping when she left. Last I saw her she was in my bedroom; she was there when I fell asleep, and when Katja woke me up she was gone."

He raised his eyes. He looked absolutely broken, which made me happy in some peculiar way. I tried to force myself not to stare just at him, but to watch others as well. Jon grinned when he realized what Henry's words implied, but then he seemed to catch himself and his smile vanished. I felt uncomfortably embarrassed that everyone on the island now knew that we had slept together, and I wondered what the Chairman would think of this little improvisation. I assumed he wouldn't appreciate it, but it was too late to do anything about that now. The colonel didn't comment on what he had just learned. Instead he said, in a neutral tone:

"And do you have any idea what the time was when you fell asleep?"

"It was after two, but probably before three."

"So that means there's a gap up until Katja found her on the ground floor around four."

I noticed that the colonel was still looking at Henry as if he wanted to ask further questions, but he didn't say any more to him; instead he began to methodically inquire how each person present had spent their evening and night. He himself had gone to bed just after midnight, and so had Lotte; Katja reported that she had done the same. When it was Jon's and Franziska's turns, they both seemed oddly unwilling to give any exact details, until it turned out that they, too, had left the group together and gone up to his room "for a nightcap," as they put it. Franziska had left his room around two, which made me gasp. I might have run into her in the hallway, which would have made everything that much more complicated.

"What kind of teenage behavior *is* all this?" Lotte exclaimed.

"I was under the impression that we had the right to a private life here," Franziska snapped back. It seemed to me that she was the least concerned of anyone in the room; she was still most irritated about how everything affected her personally.

Once everyone had given their statements, the room grew quiet again. Everyone was looking at the colonel, and I made a mental note that he was the one who had taken command of the situation. Or maybe it was more like the others had given him command. I hoped I would remember how this conversation had proceeded; my brain still felt fuzzy from the drugs, and my legs were starting to shake with the effort. I wondered how much longer I could stay in the wall without fainting, and I prayed to myself that they would soon be finished.

"Okay, this is what we're going to do," the colonel said, once he had sat in silence for a while. He rubbed his bloodshot eyes. Considering the sedative and how much he'd had to drink the evening before, he seemed surprisingly sharp and clearheaded. "It's starting to get light out. We'll divide up into two groups and search the island to find out whether we're alone or not. But before we do that I want to say two things."

The others looked at him as if he were their teacher.

"The first is that we must remain calm. We must not become frightened, because fear is the most dangerous thing of all. *No one accuses anyone of anything.* We don't know what happened, and we're not going to jump to conclusions before we find out."

He allowed his eyes to wander from one person to the next; it seemed to me that he looked at Franziska for an extra-long time.

"The second is that we must be careful. I saw Anna's body too, and from what little I know about pathology I agree with Katja. She had been strangled."

He didn't say anything for a moment and looked down before he continued.

"That means that either there are more people here on the island, or else . . ."

He cut himself short. I noticed that Lotte's eyes were large and frightened as she looked around the room at all the potential murderers. Clearly it had not occurred to her earlier that this was the most likely scenario. I hadn't expected that she would react so poorly to the situation. Emotionally shaken, slow to realize the obvious. My experience in Kyzyl Kum would have suggested otherwise, that the mothers usually handled the pressure best, while the cocky men like Jon were the ones who broke down. I wondered if she would have reacted differently if her children had been on the island, and made a mental note to include this perspective in my final report.

"What are you trying to say?" she said in a dull voice.

The colonel turned to her.

"I'm saying that none of us should be left alone. We have to stick together, all the time. We can divide up into groups, but no one goes off by himself. We keep an eye on each other. That's all we can do right now."

Inside the wall, my legs were shaking, totally out of control, and cold sweat was running down my neck and chest. My vision danced with dark spots. If I didn't sit down or get something to drink, I would pass out. The colonel's voice began to sound distant. He stood up.

"I suggest we do this: everyone goes up to his room to change clothes, but don't close the door all the way—let's make sure we can hear one another all the while. Then we'll meet back down here in five minutes and go outside together."

No one was opposed; they all began to leave the room slowly, as a group. I stayed put for a few seconds, staring out at an empty room, before I began to make my way out of the wall on wobbly legs, heading back down to my underground lair.

# # #

RIGHT FROM THE start, the secretary had admitted that there was a major shortcoming with the ancient surveillance system—I would lose contact with the participants as soon as they left the house. There was no way for me to follow them outside.

"There is a camera directly outside the front door, but it has proven impossible to put up any others. They just get blown right down," the secretary explained. Instead of arguing that he should mount his cameras a little better, I asked him what I should do if the group left the house.

"I suppose you should take the chance to recuperate," he said. When he saw my hesitant gaze, he went on: "I would seriously recommend that you follow my advice on this point. You're not going to get much sleep during these couple of days, so you'll have to get what you can in small doses when you have the chance. Go ahead and sleep if they go out. If you're able."

I just about fell face-first on the staircase down to the Strategic Level. The secretary's advice seemed so much more reasonable now than when I first heard it. I staggered to the fridge, grabbed another one of the energy drinks that took up half the space inside, and drained it in one gulp. Then I pulled over the warming blanket and sat on the floor, leaning against the wall, waiting to feel better. The trembling in my legs slowly abated, but my head still felt heavy and inert, and the soft lights and muted colors in my little bunker made me feel even more sluggish, as if I were underwater.

Once I was certain my legs would bear me, I stood up, took off everything but my underwear and camisole, crawled into the little bunk, and tried to run through and memorize everything that had just happened in the room above me. But I slowly drifted away, dozing off into half sleep where I dreamed that I, or maybe Siri, was catching crayfish in a lake where I had spent a terrible summer at camp when I was little. Nour had forced me to go, and I called home crying every day until she reluctantly agreed to come pick me up. I don't even remember if I'd actually had a bad time there; maybe it was more about a power struggle between her and me.

When she finally agreed to come get me, it had felt like a victory, but as she stepped out of her old Trabant, her mouth set in a hard line, and I stood there on the gravel with my suitcase and a resigned camp counselor, I realized that what had appeared to be a victory might have been nothing of the sort. Even then, Nour was horrible at letting bygones be bygones. The worst part was that just when I got my way and was about to go home, camp became truly fun. I had participated in a crayfish-catching expedition on the last night before Nour came. "You should at least have one good memory of camp," said Ivan, a camp counselor with kind hands and large brown eyes. One of the nice ones.

We had gone down to the shore with our flashlights, the forest dark around us, and we had emptied pot after pot. Dawn was already approaching when we walked back up to the lodge on cold legs. In my current dream, I was both myself and Siri at the same time, but every time I stuck my hand in to check for crayfish, it was like the pot expanded and became infinitely huge. I felt the crayfish moving against the back of my hand, but I could never catch hold of them. I took out my flashlight and shone it in; I could see that the trap was full of black crayfish that were crawling all over one another, but as soon as I stuck my hand in they were gone again. This went on until I heard something that dragged me back to reality. It sounded like something had fallen one floor up, inside the little medical station.

STOCKHOLM

THE   PROTECTORATE   OF   SWEDEN

MAY   2037

IT WAS THE Chairman who came through the door of the interrogation room. She stood up hastily, at a sort of attention, and her partner did the same when she shot him a look of urgency.

"I see you're surprised!" The Chairman gave a big smile and waved his hand dismissively. "By all means, have a seat. Could we have a moment alone, please? Completely alone?"

The guard nodded and left to turn off the wiretap in the room. They all sat in silence until he gave a thumbs-up through the little window in the door. The Chairman sat down across from them, in the interrogation seat.

"It wasn't my intention to shock you, dropping by unannounced like this. I really just want to wish you good luck, and make sure that we're all in agreement about these interrogations."

The Chairman absently ran his hand over his lapels, as if to brush away invisible dust or crumbs.

"In agreement?" She could tell that her colleague was

trying to make his voice sound steady, but his voice cracked like a teenage boy's. He cleared his throat. The Chairman looked at him kindly.

"Nothing dramatic at all, I just want to check in to make sure we're all on the same page as we enter the final phase of the investigation."

"What page are you on, Mr. Chairman?"

She was better than he was at handling the Chairman, who had always had a slight weakness for her. They both knew this, and that she pretended she wasn't aware. It was a practical arrangement, on her part. There were advantages. The Chairman smiled again, glad to have been handed the question he was hoping for.

"It's rather simple, isn't it? After all, it seems clear that there is one person responsible for all of this. One person who hasn't done what they should, don't you agree?"

This was what she had both expected and feared. Someone would be sacrificed. Of course. The Chairman swept his hand across the table as if gesturing at something only he could see.

"I believe," he said in a mild voice, "that this is what the investigation has shown as well, hasn't it? That certain things had not been cleared the way they should have. That things quite simply went wrong."

"But . . ." He was the one to raise his voice. She nudged him with her thigh under the table and he stopped talking. The Chairman did nothing to revive this thread of conversation. And they all sat there in silence.

"And how do you view your own role in all of this, Mr. Chairman?" she asked at last.

The Chairman looked back at her.

"Oh, wasn't it obvious when you read the preliminary investigation and the initial interviews? I knew nothing!"

Her partner gasped for breath on the chair next to hers, but she nudged him with her thigh again as a preventative measure.

"You knew nothing?" She put slight emphasis on each syllable.

"Nothing!" the Chairman said, sounding almost jolly. "Unfortunate, but not illegal. That's just what happens sometimes when you are responsible for many people and many projects all at once. You can't be aware of everything." He looked at the two of them, his eyes wandering between them. "So. Are we in agreement?"

She noticed that her colleague looked doubtful, but ignored this and gave a short nod.

"Absolutely, Mr. Chairman."

The Chairman stood up and put out his large hand first to him and then to her. She mused that it felt like taking hold of an oar.

"Excellent, then all that's left is for me to wish you both good luck with today's exercises! I look forward to reading the report later on. And now, if you'll excuse me, I have some other things to attend to."

They rose again and he left the room. She would have liked to ask him about Anna Francis, where she was now and how she was doing, and she didn't know whether it was good or bad that she had refrained. Probably good, since the Chairman himself hadn't said anything. If he'd wanted her to know, he would have informed them. She had been working closely with the RAN project for long enough to know what purpose Anna Francis had served in this game, and she wondered if

Anna herself had found out yet. She assumed that the task of explaining would fall to the Chairman.

She and her colleague found themselves standing next to each other, their eyes on the door the Chairman had just walked through. She turned to him and met his gaze.

"My God," he said quietly, dropping heavily onto his chair.

THE CHAIRMAN MOVED on through the corridor. As soon as he left the room, the smile vanished from his face. The two suit-clad bodyguards fell in behind him like shadows. The doors opened before him and closed behind him as if moved by invisible hands.

"Get the car," he said curtly to one bodyguard, who immediately veered off down the stairs, while the other waited alongside him for the elevator. The Chairman felt his suit pants squeezing a tad at the waistband, pulling a little around his thighs, and he reflected that he should start taking the stairs.

The elevator arrived and they stepped in. The bodyguard stood ahead and to the right, while he leaned against the wall behind the man.

THE ELEVATOR WHIZZED off in vacuumlike silence, and as they stepped out the other bodyguard was pulling the car up directly in front of the elevator doors. The bodyguard in the elevator walked up and opened the backseat door for the Chairman, who climbed in as he fleetingly wondered how long it had been since he'd opened a door himself. The bodyguard closed the door behind him and climbed into the front seat, and off they went.

The Chairman sank down in the black leather seat. He allowed himself to gaze out the window as they drove up out of the underground parking garage, past the checkpoints, and into the city. The gray morning clouds had blown away to reveal a lovely spring day, the type you imagine when you think of springtime, but of which there are only two or three each year. The few trees left in the city center were a fresh green, with an almost electric shimmer.

The Chairman wasn't a man prone to self-criticism, but this time he was cursing himself. There was certainly nothing wrong with the end result of the operation, *the true end result*, but he was also forced to admit that the situation had gotten out of control. He ought to have foreseen it. Too many strong wills and people acting on their own initiative. He cursed not only himself but also people in general. If only they could have stopped thinking for themselves and instead followed his instructions, it all would have been much simpler. Given the situation, he did have to accept part of the blame, at least privately. But not publicly, of course, because if this became his fault *formally* he would never be able to put it right. He stroked his lapels again, feeling the contours of what was in his inner pocket. There was a lot at stake, but he would work it out. It was up to him now.

THE CAR TURNED in at a tall, square gray building. This campus used to be called Karolinska, but many years had passed since it had occurred to anyone to pay homage to King Karl

XII and his Karoliner soldiers. Even hundreds of years after your death, you still risked being stripped of your regalia, the Chairman thought as the car slowly drove through the hospital grounds. First a national hero for a few centuries, then relabeled a dissident and enemy of the Union. The statue of Karl XII that had once stood in the Union Garden in the city center had been removed ages ago. The Chairman was old enough to recall the unrest in the 1990s, when the skinheads would gather there and pay tribute to the old warrior king, who had spent the entirety of his short adult life roving here and there with a huge army and picking fights. That sort of behavior, the Chairman thought, really ought not be so difficult for the Union leadership to understand. But of course he would never say so, if asked.

The car stopped at the security checkpoint and waited for the gates to open. Once inside, they drove past the emergency entrance and over to one of the lower wings, which protruded from the side of the large, square hulk like the leg of a crab. The car stopped outside of an unmarked entrance, and with the same coordinated motions as before, the bodyguard hopped out, opened the door for the Chairman, and fell in just behind him as they walked through the door, which silently and automatically slid up and out with such force and abruptness that the Chairman almost took it in the face.

Inside the building, the Chairman stopped to study a landscape painting in the foyer while the bodyguard approached the security window and announced their arrival. The other bodyguard had apparently been able to park the car surprisingly quickly, because he joined them after only a few minutes. An attendant soon arrived and showed the group through a number of locked doors. They walked through bright corridors with lime-green borders painted on the walls. Here and there were small conversation sets made of pale wood, with soft runners on the tabletops. Nothing here was sharp or angular, and the Chairman had the feeling of floating in a world made of butter. The attendant stopped and knocked on a door, which opened. A man with a grizzled beard peered out and was startled to find the Chairman standing outside his office.

"Hello there," the Chairman said heartily, "I just thought I'd pop by to see how our patient is doing. May I come in?"

Without waiting for an invitation, he walked past the grizzled man, his stride purposeful, and the bodyguards closed the door after them so that they were alone in the room. The grizzled man looked as if he were trying to orient himself.

"This is a bit unexpected, isn't it . . . ? But, sure, that's fine. Have a seat; there's a chair over there . . ."

The Chairman ignored his gesture toward a wooden Windsor chair in the corner of the office and instead sat down in the grizzled man's desk chair, so the man himself ended up standing in the center of the room, at a bit of a loss at what to do with himself.

"I hope I'm not disturbing you," the Chairman said, "but I thought it was about time I visited our invalid myself. I would like to have a few words with the patient, if I may?"

The grizzled man began to shake his head before the Chairman had finished his sentence.

"I don't think this is a good time. The patient is heavily sedated and still in extremely poor condition."

The Chairman squinted at him.

"Physically or mentally?"

"Both. The physical healing process is heading in the right direction, but mentally . . ." He shook his head again. The Chairman slapped both hands on his knees.

"Well, in that case it's best if I speak to the patient right away, because I have good news! I think this is something that will make the patient feel much better."

The grizzled man didn't seem convinced.

"I don't know if it's such a good idea . . ."

"Yes, it is. If a person can't even have a simple conversation about good news with your patient after weeks of care, I'll have to carefully consider sending these sorts of cases to a different unit in the future. And the subsidies with them, of course. But let's not talk about such unfortunate matters right now. I want to see the patient!"

The Chairman rose forcefully from his chair and buttoned the top button of his open jacket. The grizzled man appeared to be deliberating with himself, and then he gave a short nod. He picked up a set of keys and knocked on his own door from the inside. The bodyguard answered and let them out. The Chairman followed the man down the corridor. They stopped at a room, where the grizzled man knocked again, this time more cautiously. When there was no answer, he turned the key and stepped in. The room was empty apart from a bed, on which the shape of a body with its head toward the door was visible under the blanket. At the foot of the bed stood a table with a few wilted bouquets on it. The grizzled man approached the bed and gently shook the shoulder of the person lying there. He turned to the Chairman, his face showing relief.

"The patient is sleeping. Perhaps you can come back another day?"

"I'll stay. Everyone wakes up eventually."

The grizzled man sighed deeply. "Hold on a moment," he said, vanishing from the room and returning a minute or so later with a chair. The frame was made of a steel-like material, and the seat appeared to be covered in the same dark green linoleum as the floor. He placed it next to the bed, cracked a window, and then stood there with an uncertain expression on his face. The Chairman waved him off a bit dismissively. "This is fine. I'll let you know when I leave. I'm sure you have other things to do." It didn't quite seem like the grizzled man wanted to go, but he left the room. The Chairman sat down on the chair, ran his hand across the contents of his inner pocket once more, and, forehead wrinkled, looked at the sleeping face in the bed before him.

ISOLA

THE PROTECTORATE OF SWEDEN

MARCH 2037

ANNA

I LAY PERFECTLY still in my little bunk, listening to the sounds from the medical station, whose floor was my ceiling. A woman's voice (Katja?) shouting, *"No, no,"* more steps and thuds, and then a scream. Several loud bangs, as if heavy objects were falling to the floor, and then silence. And then steps that sounded like they were leaving the room. I spent a few seconds wondering what to do, and then I made up my mind. My legs unsteady, I struggled to rise from my cot; then I stumbled through the room and up the narrow stairs, opened the hatch, and climbed into the chest freezer. If it had been difficult to get down this way, it was nearly impossible to come back up without making noise or getting stuck. At last I managed to get into a position from which I could enter the unlock code on the control panel, which was hidden along with the hatch button in what looked like a refrigeration coil. Then, as gently as I could, I cracked the lid and peered out into the room.

It was chaos. Objects were strewn about the room as if there had been a fight. The hospital bed was overturned, and under it was Katja, who appeared lifeless. A dark red pool was expanding beneath her head at an alarming speed.

I pushed the lid open a little farther, and when it seemed the room was deserted I decided to take a chance. I awkwardly climbed out of the chest freezer and staggered over to Katja.

"Katja," I whispered. "Katja? Can you hear me?" She didn't react.

I placed a hand on her shoulder and shook her gently. Still no reaction. I kneeled down in the slippery, sticky blood to try to determine whether she was breathing, but I could neither see nor hear any inhalations, and I didn't dare try to lift her head and examine her wound while the bed was on top of her torso, pinning her to the floor, so I stood up to try to move it.

Maybe it was because my head was still heavy with the drugs, but I was too slow. I heard steps behind me and whirled around, but I was not quick enough to see who was behind me or protect myself. The blow landed hard at my temple, and everything went black.

HENRY

I FOUND THE colonel down by the little strip of sand behind the house, in the spot Anna and I had visited the night before. There he stood, staring out at the water. The wind was up to at least a moderate gale, but he didn't seem to have any trouble standing up straight. He was a large, sturdy man, but as I came closer I noticed that his shoulders were drooping.

"See anything?" I called, so he would know I was approaching from behind. He turned around, his eyes rimmed with red, watery, and swollen. He stared emptily at me, and it struck me that he must be terribly hungover. Or else he was past that stage. Longtime alcoholics often don't have such a bad time of it, or rather, they're bad off most of the time.

The colonel turned back toward the sea.

"This is so unfortunate," he said as I came up beside him. "She was a sweet girl."

Even if "sweet" wasn't the word I would have chosen to describe Anna, it was impossible to miss the sadness in his voice. It seemed reasonable that a person like the colonel

would have taken a liking to someone like Anna. Two worka-
holics. I wanted to say something but didn't know what, so I
just stood there silently in the gale. I shoved my hands as deep
into my pockets as I could and drew my shoulders up to my
ears in an attempt to shield myself from the raw cold, but it
was in vain. The gray daylight and the whipping wind, full of
tiny, salty drops of water, felt like sandpaper against my face.

"There's something about all this that doesn't add up!" the
colonel suddenly half shouted into the wind.

"What do you mean?" The wind was making my eyes tear
up as well. I wiped the corners of them with the back of my
hand. The tips of my fingers still smelled like Anna, and a series of images—her body in the darkness—passed through my
brain in a microsecond. The curve of her eyebrows. The
shape of a hip bone. The dark hollow above her collarbone,
like a bowl.

"This. All of it. This island. This death. This gathering of
people for this assignment."

He turned to me and scrutinized me, as if he were waiting
for me to say something, give him the information he was
currently lacking. When I didn't say anything, he looked
away again.

"It just doesn't add up," he said tersely.

His eyes were following Lotte, who, in her wool coat and
with her practical haircut slightly mussed, was poking around
aimlessly farther up the hill where the sparse bushes turned
into a dense and almost impenetrable thicket. Now and again
there was a gust of wind that almost dragged her a little farther
down the slope. I wondered if it was safe for her to walk up
there, or if I should call her down. In the shadow of the large

house, which towered over her with its skewed proportions, she most closely resembled an old lady who had lost her wallet rather than someone who was searching for a murderer.

"And then there's the part about the communication radio," said the colonel. "The fact that it's out of order is troubling. Very troubling. By the way, do you know what this place *is*?"

I shook my head.

"I don't either, and that concerns me too. I thought this was the sort of place I would have heard of. I won't lie, I'm starting to wonder what it was created for. Why ever would they need an inaccessible cliff with a house on top?"

"What do you think?" I asked.

"I don't think anything. But I do wonder."

"Do you know the Chairman?"

The wind carried my words away, but the colonel seemed to have understood them anyway.

"I wouldn't say I know him. But I've known *of* him for a long time. He's a climber."

The colonel spat the word.

"A climber with ambitions. Those are always the worst."

"Do you trust him?"

"No more than I trust you. Or anyone else here. Which, I would guess, is exactly how you feel?"

When I didn't respond, the colonel went on: "Just because I'm a drunkard doesn't mean I'm stupid. I notice things. About you, for example. I see what you're doing. You're doing it well. But I can see you doing it."

I felt my heart beat faster. *It doesn't mean anything, he's an old intelligence man, he sees ghosts, he suspects everyone.* I hoped my voice sounded normal when I asked him what he meant.

"Oh, I think you know," the colonel said. "You're keeping an eye out. I can tell."

He didn't seem to want to say more, and I didn't want to add to his paranoia by asking more questions. *So much for his little speech about not spreading fear and suspicion.* I wondered if it had truly been the right decision to let him take command on the island.

"What did you think when you found her?"

The question slipped out before I could stop it. I thought I had only formulated it silently in my head. I made up my mind to pay closer attention to my own symptoms of fatigue.

"At first I thought she had fallen down somehow. Maybe fainted, the same way my wife's blood pressure would often drop when she stood up, and I thought perhaps she had hit her head. But those marks on her neck . . ." His voice faded away. Neither of us made any move to leave the beach to search for an unknown killer. I realized that he also didn't think one existed.

The colonel suddenly turned to face me.

"Where did you come from, by the way?"

"I was on the other side of the house."

"Who else was there?"

"Jon and Franziska."

The colonel stared at me, his watery eyes suddenly sharp.

"Jon and Franziska?"

"Yes, we were searching the boathouse, and they seemed to have everything under control so I thought I would come down here and help you two out."

"Jon and Franziska?" he asked a third time, this time in an ever sharper tone. *"Just Jon and Franziska?"*

"Yes," I answered.

"But in that case, where's the doctor? Katja?"

My brain went perfectly still and I stared wildly back at him. Before I could open my mouth, the colonel made an about-face and began to jog up from the water's edge.

"Hold on!" I shouted after him.

"Stay there," he called to me, "keep searching the island!"

I heard him say something to Lotte on his way up, and she immediately followed him to the house. I watched them go, in the gray light, and it felt like my head was going to burst. When they were out of sight I looked at my watch, and then I, too, began to run.

ANNA

I WOKE TO the sound of an urgent buzzing. The first thing I saw was the floor, and it took me a few seconds before I figured out what was wrong with it. It was empty. No Katja. I tried to raise my head, but the pain in my temple caused it to drop back. My mind was working slowly, sluggishly. I tried again to get up, and I managed to crawl into a sitting position. Someone had tidied up the room. The bed was no longer overturned; it was back in its usual spot. The floor had been mopped clean; anyone who didn't know there had just been a large pool of blood there would never notice the faint lines the mop had left behind. And Katja was nowhere to be seen. The only odd thing about the room at that moment was that I was sitting there in my underclothes. I managed to stand up on unsteady legs. My head felt like a bowling ball and my mouth tasted like blood. Then I realized where the sound that had wakened me was coming from: someone was pressing the doorbell outside the medical station over and over again. And now they were banging on the door and yanking at its handle as well.

"Get the key from the kitchen!" I heard someone shout. It was clear that I had to get moving, make my way back down to the Strategic Level, and fast. I staggered over to the chest freezer, opened the top, and managed to climb in and close the lid after me. I desperately tried to remember the code. Nine digits. Wrong on the first try. I heard them struggling with the lock outside. My fingers shook until they almost couldn't hit the numbers. Wrong on the second try. The door to the medical station was opening. Only one chance left. The voices were in the room. A woman's voice, either Lotte's or Franziska's; it was hard to tell them apart.

"She doesn't seem to be in here."

"Are you sure?" That was the colonel.

I heard them moving around in the room. It was only a matter of time before someone lifted the lid of the chest freezer. I slowly entered the digits, my last chance. My hand was shaking uncontrollably.

"Will you check the medicine cabinet?" The colonel's voice came closer. Only three digits left.

"This is strange, don't you think, that she would disappear?" I was almost certain it was Lotte. Her voice reached me from a greater distance. She sounded shaken.

I entered the last digit and the control panel went dark. The freezer was locked. At that very moment, the lid shook. I held my breath. The colonel yanked at the lid once more.

"Yes, it's very odd, and unfortunate. Do you know how to get this open?"

The interior control panel lit up, right next to my face. I realized he was trying out different codes, and I hoped they were random. As far as I knew, Katja and I were the only ones who could lock and unlock the freezer, but Katja had disappeared and I didn't know where she was, only that someone out there had cleared her out of the way. If it was the colonel, maybe he had gotten her to give up the codes. His hands were scratching at the control panel just inches from my face. I held my breath.

"I can't find anything here. Should we deal with the kitchen now?" That was Lotte.

I heard the colonel stand up; the control panel went dark and his steps left the room. So whoever had attacked Katja had managed to stash her on the island somewhere, out of the way, given that the others seemed to be searching for her. That same person was likely the one who struck me in the head. Someone out there knew I hadn't died last night after all.

I lay where I was for a moment, breathing and going through my options. It occurred to me that the person who had attacked Katja and me might be hiding on the Strategic Level, along with Katja. If that was the case, I would be throwing myself right into his or her arms if I climbed down there right away. But it seemed even more dangerous to go the other direction, and remaining in the freezer box until the rescuers arrived from the mainland seemed like the worst option. So I decided to go down there after all.

As quietly and cautiously as possible, I sneaked down the steep staircase. The room downstairs was empty, just as I had left it. I hoped that meant Katja and I were still the only ones who knew about the Strategic Level and how to get there. My knees were still dark with dried blood and I dampened a towel to clean them off. Then I placed the towel in a bag and taped it shut, in case it could somehow be used for evidence. There were drugs on the shelf above me, and with a certain amount of effort I reached for the bottle of painkillers, shook out three, and took them. My mouth was dry, and I had to swallow hard several times to get them down. The taste of medicine lingered in my mouth as I sat down at the screens on the other side of the room. I tried to force away thoughts of Katja and what her disappearance might mean, but it was hard. Should I interrupt my own assignment and look for her? I was hesitant. My instructions said that I must not reveal myself *no matter what happened*. I decided that I might have a better chance of finding Katja by looking for her from my current location and with the tools I had available: the screens and the walls.

I began to go through the grainy images I had at my disposal, screen by screen. On the ground floor, I could see Lotte and the colonel methodically searching through both the kitchen and the parlor; upstairs I could see Jon and Henry jogging down the hall and opening the doors into all the rooms. Franziska was standing near the stairs, her arms crossed, and it didn't appear that she was saying or doing anything at all. Her small, grainy, greenish-blue silhouette looked very cold; you could see that much even on my pixelated screen, because she pulled her fur-trimmed coat closer around herself again and again, as if it didn't cover her thoroughly enough. The three of them eventually vanished out of sight of the upstairs hallway camera and instead showed up again on the one that captured the great hall. They went into the kitchen, where everyone was now gathered, and in order to hear what was being said I hurried to stand up, open the narrow door, and follow them, back into the wall.

# # #

"How could this happen? I thought she was with you."

Lotte's voice cracked; it sounded like she was on the verge of a breakdown.

"People have to be responsible for themselves, don't they? She was with us when we went out, I'm sure of that, and it's not my job to keep track of where everyone is," Franziska snapped back. She was leaning against the kitchen chair Jon had sunk down onto. He was really starting to look rotten. He was probably also terribly hungover, like the colonel, and he was leaning heavily forward on his chair, as if he were on the toilet.

Franziska, however, looked as if she had recovered from the initial shock and had gathered new strength. She had somehow found time to fix herself up and dress in a well-coordinated outfit. She had taken off her coat and under it she was wearing wide black trousers and a bright pink tie-front cardigan with some sort of colorful pattern, the kind that looks hand-knitted but is in fact ridiculously expensive, probably imported. It was the sort of outfit she might have selected for an in-home interview in a women's magazine, seemingly effortless and casual.

Now that I could observe her undisturbed, I noticed that there was a strange little indentation on her throat just below her chin, and that the skin around her eyes seemed too tight when she spoke. Plastic surgery, presumably. There were rumors that the top party members and other dignitaries had their own clinic, and American cosmetic surgeons were flown in to cut on the country's best for sky-high fees and in the utmost secrecy. I wondered if Franziska had been there. Maybe her brother-in-law in the Department of the Interior had arranged the operations. That was how it usually worked. I heard Nour's loud, resonant snort in my head. She had always hated that sort of vanity and shallowness with a fervor that made me wonder if it was really a matter of jealousy.

It struck me that Nour and Franziska must have moved in the same circles once upon a time, and I wondered if they knew each other. It wasn't impossible. Maybe Franziska had been one of those who sat around in Nour's apartment in Hökarängen, cigarette smoke stinging her eyes and her vodka glass constantly refilled, singing party songs and discussing politics as I lay in the next room with a pillow over my head, trying to sleep. I would have liked to ask Franziska about this, if only to see her reaction, but now it was too late. And whatever she'd done in her youth, she had obviously maneuvered her way up through the party apparatus better than Nour, considering her current position. If you were to place her and Nour side by side today, it would be clear that Franziska was the success story. It was really only the reserved look in her eyes that spoke to something different.

THE CONVERSATION ABOUT what might have happened to Katja flowed back and forth in the room.

"How do we know she didn't leave the island?" This was Jon, lifting his head with great effort.

"There's no way," the colonel said wearily. "You checked the boathouse, right? As far as I'm aware, there is no boat here that is seaworthy enough to take her any great distance in this gale."

"Then could someone have picked her up?"

Apparently Jon didn't really want to let his theory go. The colonel continued to contradict him. His tone of voice made him sound like he was talking to an unruly child who refused to listen.

"If she had been picked up by helicopter, we would have noticed. This island is too small for anyone to land without everyone seeing it."

"Maybe she's hiding of her own volition."

"Why on earth would she do that?" Franziska snapped.

It occurred to me that, up to this point, I had heard her use only two tones of voice. The cheerful one, which she had used on Jon at dinner last night, and this snappish, displeased one, which seemed to be her normal mode of conversation. Jon looked at her.

"I don't know . . . Maybe she's afraid. Maybe she knows something we don't."

Jon took a deep breath and went on:

"Maybe she knows who the killer is and she's keeping away from him . . ."

"Or her," Lotte interjected.

"Or her," Jon conceded. "Or maybe she's even the one who . . . She *was* the one who found Anna's body, wasn't she? How do we know she didn't strangle her and then . . ."

He looked at the others to garner support for his theory, which he seemed to find more appealing the longer he spoke. His voice grew firmer and more didactic; it was obvious once more that he was used to being listened to. "It's totally plausible. She murders Anna, locks up the body so the rest of us can't examine it, and then goes into hiding. I consider this a reasonable scenario, and I think we ought to start acting accordingly."

"The floor," the colonel said quietly.

The others turned around and looked at him.

"What?" Jon said.

"The floor," the colonel said again, a bit louder this time. "It looked as if someone had mopped the floor. From what I could determine, someone had wiped up blood."

He took a white handkerchief from his pocket and held it up. One side was rusty brown. Everyone else in the room looked at the handkerchief in confusion, and the colonel suddenly seemed to realize that they didn't understand what he was showing them. "When I was down in the doctor's office with Lotte, I noticed it looked like someone had wiped something off the floor. So I took a handkerchief and wiped a little more, and I think . . ."

He steeled himself.

"I think this is blood, and if it is, it's reasonable to assume it came from Katja. Which means she was bleeding on the floor, and someone—or maybe she herself—later mopped it up. So as it stands now, it seems most plausible that someone harmed her and then cleaned up afterward. But we don't know this. At the moment, I can see no good reason for why Katja would harm herself, then clean up after herself and disappear. Occam's razor, my friends. That means . . ."

"What is likely is the truth. Yes, I know, no need to lecture me." Franziska sighed.

The colonel seemed to take no notice of her sarcasm; instead he went on: "This is what we have right now. We have nothing more. We know nothing more."

"That could be any old dirt," Jon said, but there wasn't much weight to his voice anymore.

"Incidentally, I tested the communication radio while I was down there," the colonel said. "Still dead."

Henry said nothing. He seemed fully occupied with pouring coffee into an insulated carafe. A strangely old-lady-like gesture, instead of serving it directly out of the coffeemaker carafe. When he started going around and pouring coffee into the others' cups, he looked like one of the servants. I had noticed earlier that he had a way of making himself invisible sometimes, and I knew he did it on purpose, when he would rather listen than speak. A thrill ran through my body when I looked at him, a longing to walk right through the wall and place my nose behind his ear, my arms around his waist.

He, too, looked cold and tired as he walked around with his carafe. I would have given anything to be lying around on a bed somewhere with him, hungover and watching old movies. Just as I had this thought, an uncanny certainty flowed through me and told me that this would never happen. It made me want to cry.

"What's more," the colonel said, aiming a strict look at Jon, "I think we should be very careful about forming theories of guilt in this matter. If this turns into a witch hunt we are doomed; it is very important that we all remember that." Franziska immediately raised more objections.

As I stood there listening to them argue back and forth about what to do next, with not just one but two people missing and possibly dead, and how they would go about arranging a more thorough search of the house itself, I happened to be reminded that there actually was another way to communicate with the outside world, besides the communication radio in the medical station. Lotte's satellite phone. The one I had seen her speaking on the night before. I watched as she paced back and forth across the room. Unlike Jon and Franziska, she wasn't extravagantly clad in the least. The only aberration from her plain style was the large, shiny leather handbag she held on to almost desperately with both hands as she walked back and forth. To the window. To a chair. I assumed the satellite phone was in the bag and that was why she carried it with her at all times.

I had received clear instructions from the secretary that my task was to observe and nothing more. Whatever happened, I was not to interfere in the course of events. But then again, the course of events had interfered with me in a way I wondered if the secretary had really foreseen. For one thing, I was now, to some extent, found out. Someone on the island knew that I had not in fact died on the first night and had done their best to neutralize me. Since my body hadn't been discovered, he or she must also have realized that this had failed, and that I was still on the island, possibly hurt but still alive. For another, Katja was missing now too, and if she wasn't dead she was at least seriously injured. There had been a lot of blood on the floor. I wondered if I ought to climb out of my hiding spot and tell the others what I knew, but I decided it was safer to keep hidden. So far, no one but me seemed to know that the Strategic Level existed or how to get into it, so I had that on my side for the time being. Furthermore, I considered the Chairman's threat in the conference room on the fourteenth floor. Cutting the assignment short would have consequences I preferred not to think about. But maybe there was another possibility: I could try to contact the secretary, I thought as I watched Lotte hug her bag to her body as if it were a heating pad.

The colonel suddenly pressed his hands to his knees and stood up laboriously.

"We need to search the house again, thoroughly. If Katja is hiding or being hidden somewhere in this house, she must be seriously injured. I suggest we split up."

"I think we might need to have breakfast as well," Henry said calmly.

"Good. True." The colonel cast him a grateful look. "You and Lotte stay down here, go through the ground floor first, and if you don't come up with anything you can start preparing breakfast; the rest of us will search the rest of the house together as carefully as we possibly can. And let's pray to God we find Katja before it's too late."

With that, he gave Franziska and Jon an urgent look and then left the kitchen along with everyone else.

I wondered how to handle the situation now that the group had divided into two, and in the end I decided to go down by the cameras so I would have an overview of everyone at the same time. For the next half hour, with the help of the screens, I studied the way the two groups searched and searched, in locations both likely and unlikely, how Lotte and Henry searched first the kitchen and then the parlor; then they moved on to all the cabinets and every nook and cranny between the two, while the colonel, Jon, and Franziska searched the upstairs rooms. Lotte carried her bag with her the whole time, into every room, putting it down only when she needed both hands. I thought I caught Henry sneaking a look at the bag once in a while when Lotte was busy elsewhere, and I assumed he was also thinking about the satellite phone. Maybe he was looking for the chance to take it out of the bag, or maybe he was just curious about it the same way I was. By all appearances, he never brought it up with Lotte, and eventually they stopped their search and vanished into the kitchen to prepare breakfast. After a while, the upstairs group joined them and I left the screens and followed them back into the kitchen wall. Not that there was much to listen to. The five people in the kitchen began to eat their breakfast under oppressive silence; all the while, the gray light outdoors slid imperceptibly into late morning, and the wind grew stronger.

SUDDENLY HENRY STOOD up and walked over to the window. He turned to the others.

"What is that, moving out there?"

The colonel came to stand beside him and looked out.

"I don't know; can someone hand me the binoculars? I thought I saw a pair in the hall."

Lotte rose and vanished out of my sight, returning after a moment with a pair of binoculars, which she passed to the colonel. He put them to his eyes and gave a little cry.

"What on earth—that's the pier!"

Everyone darted from their chairs; the colonel grabbed his jacket and hurtled out the door. The others followed. Left behind, next to Lotte's chair, was her handbag.

I realized that this was my chance, now or never.

WHEN I WAS totally certain that everyone had left the house to run down to the pier, I made my way through the chest freezer again and came up into the medical station. Without really thinking about what I was about to do, I hurried over to the shelf of medicine, found what I was looking for, and tucked the bottle in my pocket. Then I rushed out of the room. The house felt enormous now that no one else was in it. I ran into the kitchen, crouching so that I wouldn't be visible through the window. I snatched Lotte's large bag and had to fiddle with the closure mechanism for a moment before I got it open. She seemed to be the sort of person who kept everything but the kitchen sink in her bag. Wallet, keys, gum, printed bus schedule, tampons, Band-Aids, receipts held together with a paper clip, a half-eaten piece of chocolate, bobby pins, a dog-eared child's drawing that depicted some sort of orange blob, a bracelet that looked like it had been purchased at a cheap trinket store.

When I was little, Nour had a large briefcase she always carried with her. I wasn't allowed to look inside it, which might be why I loved digging through it when she wasn't paying attention. It was like a secret lexicon, a way to understand her.

I gathered evidence, receipts from places she'd had coffee or items she had bought; I looked through her calendar to find out who she had met with. True to her paranoid ways, she often didn't write down exact information, just an initial or a time. I stored all of this in my memory, collecting it in my inner war chest, as if I needed information I could hold over Nour although I didn't quite know why.

I went through Lotte's bag in the same methodical manner, even though I realized right away that the satellite phone wasn't there. I pocketed one of her bobby pins, closed the bag again, and put it aside. I cautiously looked out the window to make sure that no one was on their way back up to the house. Then I sneaked out of the kitchen, up the stairs, and down the hallway. I counted the doors on the left until I arrived at Lotte's. I was prepared to pick the lock with the bobby pin (a skill I'd learned back in my childhood and later honed in Kyzyl Kum), but it turned out that the door was unlocked, so I stepped in. The light inside was dim, the blinds halfway closed and clothes tossed everywhere. A pair of white cotton panties, clearly used, were crumpled up in a pair of nylons, and the bed was unmade, as though someone had just thrown off the covers and run away. That was presumably exactly what had happened. If I'd felt unreal when I was sneaking around inside the walls, I was almost panicked now. It was in every way socially repellent to walk around a stranger's room, digging through her clothes and belongings, through her wardrobe, through her bathroom. I felt like a crazy person, someone who had crossed a line. And even though I had been hiding for only half a day, it felt unnatural to stand in the middle of a room, fully visible, instead of hiding in a dark corridor. I took a deep breath, pulled myself together, and began my search.

I went through the room as methodically as I could, and now and then I cast a glance out the window. The others seemed fully occupied down by the cliff's edge, and I crossed my fingers that they would be gone for a while longer. It took an unreasonably long time to search her room; my hands were still clumsy from the drugs Katja had given me hours before and from the blow to my head. Several times I found myself standing there with something in my hand, without really knowing how it had come to be there or how long I had been standing that way. I tried to be strategic and went so far as to look under the lid of the toilet tank, but no matter how hard I searched I couldn't find the phone. Of course, it was possible that she had it on her, hidden on her body somewhere, but I thought it was unlikely since the phone was rather large and bulky. Carrying it around like that would be asking for someone to discover it. But suddenly another thought struck me. There was someone else who knew about Lotte's phone—someone whose room shared a wall with hers.

Henry.

HENRY'S ROOM WASN'T locked either, and I stood in the doorway for a moment before I walked in. The room looked different in daylight, but one thing was the same: there was barely any evidence that he had been there. Unlike Lotte's feverish absence, this room was as tranquil as a monastery cell. There was nothing in the room to indicate that he was staying there, that *anyone* was staying there, really. The bed was made as if by hotel staff, the sheets taut, and all belongings were stashed away, except for a paperback on the nightstand. I started by looking under the bed, where I found his empty suitcase. Apparently he had unpacked everything he'd brought with him, and then primly placed the plain, navy blue suitcase, with its filled-out luggage tag, under the bed.

For reasons I didn't quite understand myself, I found his neatness exasperating. I walked over to the wardrobe and opened it. His clothes, too, were arranged in perfect order. A pair of brown leather shoes on the floor. Two blazers. Dark pants. Freshly ironed shirts on hangers; a couple of undershirts. On a shelf lay two knitted sweaters in shades that recalled construction material. I recognized one of them from the first night. This unremarkable orderliness irritated me as well, but strangely enough, I also found it attractive. There was something sensual about looking at his clothes, touching them. Clothes that had lain against his skin, touched his chest, his arms. I put out my hand and stroked a blue-gray shirt, then bent forward to sniff it. There was a scent of fabric softener. The creases on the sleeves were so well ironed that they were almost sharp, and I absently wondered if he ironed his shirts himself or took them to a dry cleaner.

Digging around in Henry's wardrobe made me feel like I had the upper hand somehow, as if I could finally observe him as much as I wanted and he wouldn't even know. I lifted up the sweater from our first evening and inhaled its scent. It smelled faintly of aftershave and human.

For a split second I wondered if I should take it with me, but I quickly realized the absurdity in taking that sort of risk. I put the sweater back where it belonged and continued to browse through everything else at random. And then I found it. Behind the clothes was a cabinet that extended right into the wall. The door resembled that of a safe, but I tried it out and it wasn't locked; I was able to open it. And even though it was pretty dark in the wardrobe, I saw right away what the cabinet contained. There was a bundle of papers—a personal dossier—with a photocopy of my passport on the front. And a pistol.

I RECOILED AS if the door to the cabinet had burned me, and I let out a little screech. I took a few quick steps toward the window; to my dismay, I found that the others had started to make their way back up to the house, and quickly. Without really knowing why, I grabbed the gun from the cabinet, closed the safe door, pulled the clothes back in front of it, closed the wardrobe, left the room, and hurried back down the stairs. I heard the front door opening just as I was climbing into the chest freezer. Someone called, "Go down and get the warming blanket!" Steps were approaching; this time I managed to lock the chest on the first try. I lay as still as I could, heart pounding, as I heard someone rummaging around the room, clearly in a hurry. The person appeared to find what they were looking for, and I heard their steps jogging off and the door closing. I tried to focus by slowly counting to one hundred. Then I began my arduous journey through the hatch. I tried to move as silently as I could down the narrow stairs, and then I was back in my underground room, panting, the gun heavy in my hand.

HENRY

"WHERE IS HE? Where is he?" Lotte was shouting right next to my ear. It took every ounce of self-control to keep myself from telling her to shut up. Instead I kept fighting my way up the ladder in my ice-cold, heavy clothing; once I was up I fell on my back and tried to catch my breath again. I undid the clasp on my wet and unwieldy life jacket and wriggled out of it, then rolled onto my side and coughed. Salt water poured out of my mouth as I heaved. I rested my forehead on the muddy, trampled grass and tried to breathe normally. I almost hadn't made it back to land.

ABOUT FIFTEEN MINUTES earlier, we had all run down to the pier. Or, rather, to the lawn by the ladder, above the spot where the pier had once been. At the moment, the pier itself was rapidly floating away from land. Without it, a larger boat would never be able to dock, at least as long as the bad weather lasted. Which would mean we were truly isolated.

"We have to try and get it!" I shouted to the others. The wind had whipped up even harder, and if this continued it would soon be a true storm. The rain was lashing sideways.

"There's a rubber boat in the boathouse," Jon called.

"Go get it!" I shouted back, and he returned a minute or two later, dragging a large, inflatable navy-style dinghy with a tiny outboard motor. When the wind caught it, it almost hurled him over the cliff. Lotte dashed over to help him, and together they began to lower it down. The wind tossed it about, and it nearly knocked me off the ladder a couple of times. Once I made it down to the thin strip of beach, I took hold of it with difficulty and managed to set it in the water in the little lee afforded by the cliff.

"Are you coming?" I called to the colonel. He looked at me hesitantly, but then he made up his mind and began to climb down. Jon made a move as if to follow him.

"It'll be too heavy! Wait here!"

Jon stopped on the first rung of the ladder and climbed back over the top. A flicker of relief washed over his face. The colonel stepped into the boat, stooped past me, and sat in the stern. I took the oars from the bottom of the boat; once we had struggled to row a few meters away from the cliff wall I turned on the motor, and then we steered out onto the choppy sea and toward the pier, which was floating farther and farther away on the waves.

Once we were at a safe distance from the sharp rocks and definitely out of earshot, I adjusted my position, hoping to use my back to block the others from seeing us.

"I have to talk to you," I half shouted to him, turning off the motor and moving closer.

⧉ ⧉ ⧉

ONCE I'D SAID what I had to say, I took a deep breath and awaited the colonel's reaction. His gaze was steady as he looked into my eyes. There was nothing left of his watery, absent gaze, and I realized how much respect he must have commanded earlier in his life. He was a man who knew what had to be done.

"Are you absolutely certain about this?" he asked.

"Absolutely certain," I said, hoping it would turn out to be true.

He looked away, gazing at the beach and letting out a small laugh.

"I'll be damned," he said.

Then his body swayed, and with a deft motion, as if he had done this many times before, he overturned the boat and we both went into the ice-cold water.

ANNA

ONCE I HAD calmed down in my basement it became clear to me that it had truly not been a stroke of genius to take the gun. I risked rousing Henry's suspicions, because of course the weapon couldn't have taken itself from the cabinet, as he would doubtless realize. But—and I couldn't keep these uncomfortable questions at bay any longer—why did Henry have a gun, and why did he have a file about me? And why hadn't I taken that too, as long as I was taking the gun?

I cursed myself for having thought both quickly and slowly at the same time. Apparently Henry was not just a candidate for the position; his presence on the island seemed to have something to do with me. Without really reflecting on it, I had assumed all along that I could trust him, had assumed we were on the same team. But the sight of the gun and the personnel file together in the cabinet, hidden behind his clothes, felt like finding a back door into his brain, and what I found inside was something I had neither wished for nor expected.

I placed the gun on the desk before me and began to

inspect it. It was a type of handgun I hadn't seen before, but that didn't really mean anything, since the only guns I'd seen up close were old Mauser rifles, revolvers, and Soviet AK-47s belonging to the military in Kyzyl Kum. This gun looked nothing like those; it looked much more modern. It was slim and mechanical with bullets in a magazine; there were none of the rustic details I associated with civilian hunting weapons. I thought it looked much more military in nature. I knew Henry had once been in the military, of course; he had told me so himself long ago as we discussed the project that paved the way for the trip to Kyzyl Kum. But many people had that sort of background; it didn't necessarily mean anything. Unless he was still part of it. *A spy?* I took a sharp breath. There had always been something unusual about his reticence, something that seemed almost pathological. Or professional. I thought about his ridiculously neat room, his plain dress, his discretion. The fact that I really didn't know anything about him but the few things he had told me himself. Until now. My thoughts whirled every which way. It was impossible to say whether I was being paranoid or naive; I had nothing useful to compare this to. There were no guidelines, no conventions, for how to react in this sort of situation.

I sat down and stared apathetically at the screens, the gun before me, and was trying to figure out what to do next when the whole group abruptly popped up on one screen as they darted into the front hall. Although it wasn't quite the whole group, I realized suddenly. The colonel was missing. There was no time to wonder why, because Henry headed straight for the stairs, apparently on his way up to his room. I made my way into the wall space, ran as quietly and quickly as I could up the padded stairs in the wall, and entered his room just after he did—but in the viewing area. The first thing he did was shuck out of his soaked clothes. He yanked and tore at them as if he couldn't get them off fast enough. Garment after garment, until he was standing in the room naked. It was hard to comprehend that we had slept together less than twenty-four hours previously; his body looked both foreign and familiar in the gray daylight. I could see now that he had a number of scars on his body: a long one on his thigh and what looked like old gunshot wounds on his chest, dangerously close to his heart. I had felt the scars on his chest the day before, but I had been too engrossed in him to really pay attention to them. He walked into the bathroom. I heard the shower come on. I began to move so that I could follow him along the wall. I stood there indecisively for a moment, without opening the peephole. It felt peculiar to watch strangers through the wall, but that was nothing compared to how it felt to try to chase Henry into the bathroom without his knowledge. But it wasn't only reluctance that was making me feel out of sorts. I *wanted* to see Henry in the shower, and I felt ashamed of it. I started searching for the hatch in the wall with my fingertips, but no matter how much I groped around in the dark I couldn't find it. There was no peephole. At first I felt frustrated and almost a little angry, and then I was concerned. Had Henry been placed in a room where he couldn't be observed in the bathroom on purpose? Was he aware of this? And what did all of this have to do with the gun? I tried to listen through the wall, but all I could hear was the sound of the shower, pounding with that irregular yet rhythmic sound that is created when jets of water break against a body moving slowly beneath them.

⁜ ⁜ ⁜

EVENTUALLY HE TURNED off the shower and came back out of the bathroom with a white towel around his waist. I had no view of the wardrobe from my lookout, yet I could hear him rooting around in it, presumably going after clothes. But then the sound changed, as if his movements grew more spasmodic. He took a step back, staring wild-eyed around the room. I couldn't interpret this in any other way but that he had realized the gun was missing. He tossed all his clothing out of the wardrobe, then tore the sheets off the bed, took out his suitcase, threw it on top of his clothes, and rummaged through everything. The sight was almost comical. He even looked under the paperback novel on the nightstand out of sheer desperation. At last he appeared to give up. He sat on the edge of the bed for a moment, staring emptily at nothing. He sat that way for almost a minute, and then he seemed to come to some decision; he grabbed a pair of underwear from the pile of clothes, dressed hurriedly, and left the room. I followed him, inside the walls.

THE LAST TIME they took Nour in was after Grandpa got sick. This was a few years after he had moved back home. It had been a long process to get permission to emigrate, because Bosnia was no longer part of the Union, but at last they let him go. He had never been all that active in the party, and when it became clear that he was prepared to relinquish his pension, they probably realized that it would be more profitable to be rid of him. I don't know whether Nour grieved over him then, because she didn't say anything. It didn't become a problem until he got sick. Nour wanted to travel to see him, but she wasn't allowed. "You are needed here," they said. "We can't allow so much knowledge to leave the country," they said. They were afraid she would defect. This was after I had moved out, so I didn't see much of it, but I know she handed in application after application. "REQUEST TO CARE FOR DYING PARENT," it read in angry red letters on one of the envelopes she sent in; I saw it lying in her hallway, ready to be mailed. Even then, I suspected that things weren't going well for her when it came to an exit visa, and I knew there had already been a schism between her and the party, but I don't think I understood how desperate she truly was.

One day I received a strange phone call from Nour. She asked me to pick her up at home and take her to the hospital. This was unlike her; she usually made it a matter of pride never to be sick. When I got to her building, the door was unlocked, and her apartment smelled close and musty. I called for her, but there was no response. The dishes in the kitchen sink looked like they had been there for many days. On the kitchen table was a tub with some dried-out butter on the bottom. I tiptoed up to her bedroom. Nour was in bed, sleeping. I hadn't seen her asleep since I was a child. Her features were soft and peaceful; the wrinkle between her eyebrows was smooth. But otherwise she looked horrible. Her face was pale, bordering on olive green, and the skin of her arms looked several sizes too big. She must have been sick for a long time. The room smelled sweet with unwashed body, and on the floor next to the bed were glasses, cups, plates, and tons of empty packets of painkillers. I sat down on the edge of the bed and placed my hand on her arm. I didn't know whether I should wake her up, but after a little while it seemed she sensed my presence in the room. She turned her head drowsily and looked at me.

"Anna?" She seemed surprised at first.

"How long have you been sick?"

Nour looked at me as if she didn't quite understand what I was saying.

"How long have you been sick?" I asked again.

She cleared her throat a little. I handed her a glass of water, the one I thought looked freshest. She took it and raised her head to drink, then sank back down and looked at me.

"Anna, you have to help me get to the hospital. I need to be inspected."

"Examined," I corrected her. "You need an examination. You're sick."

She shook her head, annoyed.

"No, no, they have to inspect me. I'm going to go on early disability retirement."

She looked determined. Her usual little wrinkle between the eyebrows was back. I didn't understand.

"Nour, you're just sick; why would they put you on disability?"

"They have to," she said, pressing her lips together like a stubborn child. "They have to now."

Suddenly I understood. I shivered.

"No" was all I said.

"Yes," she said, looking resolutely into my eyes.

We sat there for a long time, our eyes fixed on each other.

I had heard of this before, how people would go to extremes to render themselves useless to the party in order to get an exit permit. But I thought those were only urban legends.

"Sit up so I can take a look," I said.

"You don't have to," Nour replied. "They can do that at the hospital."

"I want to. Please sit up."

Reluctantly, and with great effort, Nour sat up in bed. I pulled up her nightgown. There was a stained compress taped to her lower back. A sour smell emanated from it. I cautiously loosened the tape, and she mewled a little as the sticky surfaces let go of her skin. Little gray outlines remained where the tape had been. The wound from which they had removed far too much spinal fluid was in the very center of her spine, between two vertebrae, and it was weeping pus.

"Stay there; I'm going to wash it."

Nour didn't protest, she just breathed heavily, so I went into the bathroom, wet some toilet paper with lukewarm water, rooted around the medicine cabinet until I found something that would work as a compress, and went back to the bedroom. She was just as I had left her. Nour's black hair hung across her face; I couldn't see her expression.

"I have trouble walking," she said suddenly. "You have to hold me up."

"How are you feeling otherwise? Does anything else hurt?"

"My head," Nour said. "But that's to be expected."

"Couldn't you just have dropped an iron on your foot instead?" I said, stroking her hair gently. Nour shook her head.

"Don't be stupid. Broken bones can heal. It has to be permanent."

I washed her wound carefully. It looked horrible. I thought about asking who had done it, but I knew she wouldn't tell me and that this was probably for the best. That person might get into trouble; I might too if I knew.

"You're an idiot," I said in a soft voice.

She was, of course. But still.

"He's my father," she said quietly. "I can't let him die alone."

I put on the fresh compress and stroked her back. Then I adjusted the pillows so that the softest one would land right under her spine.

"You can lie back down," I said.

She sank back with a sigh. She looked at me, her expression stern.

"I would have done the same for you, I want you to know. And you would too, for me. It's the only decent thing to do."

"I know," I said.

Then I didn't say anything more; I just sat there on the edge of the bed for a while.

At the hospital, of course, there was a scene. The first doctor who examined her called in a second. Then the security police arrived. I was taken to another room, one without windows, where eventually a person in uniform, someone whose position was unclear, interrogated me for hours. Had I known what she was planning to do? Did I know who had performed the procedure? Did I know why she had done it? There was no point in refusing to answer this last question, because I knew based on their questions that they had figured it out, so I told it like it was: I believed it was connected to the fact that Grandpa was sick in Bosnia, and she wanted to be put on disability pension so she could travel there and take care of him.

They bludgeoned me with the same questions and answers again and again, with few or no variations. Eventually I was standing outside the hospital, in the sleet, and I was allowed to go home, without having been allowed to see Nour again.

I later learned that they had moved her to the prison hospital, and that she stayed there for six weeks. They also told her (and this didn't come out until much later either) that I had given her up. Six weeks later, when I called the prison, they suddenly informed me that she was back home again. And it was true. With her disability pension and on crutches. By that time Grandpa was already dead, and Nour would be a dissident forever after, a dissident who would need a crutch wherever she went. We never spoke of all this again, but I think about it often. The things you do for your own.

I SAW MANY mutilated people in Kyzyl Kum. Moms mutilated their sons to keep them at home; men shot themselves in the legs or feet to avoid battle. I saw so many dead bodies that it almost, but only almost, became ordinary. Some were strangers; others were painfully close to me; some were so maimed that I almost felt relieved that they wouldn't have to live in such a condition, while others just looked like they were sleeping. Some were old; others were far too young. But it had never occurred to me that there might be times when it would be a welcome sight to have a dead body there in front of you, that being certain would actually be preferable to this scenario: having two people vanish on an island in the middle of nowhere, with no bodies to be found. At least, this was how I understood the situation as I listened to Franziska, Jon, Lotte,

and Henry sit in the parlor and attempt to make head or tails of what had just happened. The colonel had vanished into the water when the boat overturned, and now it was too stormy to go out on the water and search for him. Not to mention that the boat was missing. We were truly isolated now. Jon didn't seem satisfied with the answers he was getting from Henry.

"But what did he say while you were out there?"

"We were just talking about what might have happened to the pier, how it could have come unmoored."

"And what conclusion did you come to?"

"Well, there was no way to tell until we got to it and examined it, but I suppose there was . . . a certain amount of suspicion that someone might have loosened it."

"Why would someone have loosened it?"

Henry stopped staring at the invisible spot he seemed to have been studying up to that point and turned to look at Jon.

"To isolate us, of course. Now we can't get out of here. It's no longer possible to come in by boat, at least not until the wind dies down."

"But . . ."

Henry went on, showing no mercy: "In which case, someone on this island really does mean to harm the rest of us. But there's still no way for us to know for certain, just as we don't know whether the pier detached itself or whether it was actually the colonel who murdered Anna, made Katja disappear, and then sabotaged the pier. Because now he's gone too, and the boat is gone, and the communication radio in the basement doesn't work . . ."

Jon interrupted him.

"And whose fault is it that the boat and the colonel are

gone? Are you just going to stand here running your mouth when it's your fault that . . ."

"If you have any suggestions about how we should solve this, I'm all ears," Henry said stiffly.

No one said anything. The room seemed unusually still. Franziska was the one to break the silence. For the first time she sounded neither offended nor ingratiating, just exhausted.

"We're all tired. And in shock, I assume. I am, at least. I suggest we attempt to eat something and get some rest, and after that we'll try to compose ourselves and figure out what to do."

This was a reasonable suggestion, and as she uttered it I realized I hadn't eaten for many hours either. My legs felt thick and swollen, and I was weak and hungry. As the others got organized (Franziska and Jon decided to go to the kitchen to get out the food; Henry and Lotte stayed in the parlor to make a fire and set the table), I staggered down to my basement and over to the fridge. I made a monster of a sandwich, with everything on it, and then I ate the whole thing in thirty seconds, in the yellowish light of the lamp, my eyes half on the grainy screens. Franziska and Jon eventually joined Lotte and Henry back in the parlor.

The scene was almost cozy as they sat before the fire in their easy chairs, eating sandwiches and serving themselves tea from a beautiful samovar. Afterward, they lingered there. I assumed they all felt drained. Now and then I went up in the passageway and listened to see if anything interesting was being discussed, but they mostly didn't speak. No one suggested that they go out and resume the search. Most of them seemed to have settled on waiting the whole thing out. Everyone but

Franziska had selected a book from the large bookcase, and they seemed thoroughly absorbed in reading, while Franziska alternately sat on the sofa beside Jon and stared listlessly at the fire on the one hand and restlessly paced the room and stared out the window at the sea on the other, all while the sun set. At one point, Henry and Jon went down to the medical station to test the communication radio. By now the wind appeared to be blowing at a full gale, and it tore and clawed at the house until the windows rattled.

It was hardly past nine o'clock at night when Franziska and Jon said they were going to go to bed and left the room. Soon thereafter, Lotte and Henry also left the ground floor and went up to their respective rooms. When I checked in on them all a little while later, they appeared to have gone to bed. Jon was on the sofa in Franziska's room; the others were in their own beds. I decided to get some sleep as well, so I crawled into the bunk and set my alarm to wake me a few hours later, with the goal of getting up and checking in on everyone. I barely had time to lay my head on the hard, flat pillow, pull the gray army blanket over myself, and muse that it was a damn shame that everything in the military had to be so uncomfortable before I faded away into sleep, down into a well of darkness.

I WAS BACK in Kyzyl Kum. Although it was dark around me, I knew where I was at once. The raw, cold night air, the odor of brown coal burning in a stove, the sound of the wind beating against tents. Flap flap flap. It was nighttime. I was wearing my sleeping mittens and my hat since the stove was unreliable and you never knew if you would wake shivering with cold. But that wasn't why I was awake. There was someone moving around in the hospital tent. Not the usual stirrings of people tossing and turning with cold or pain on their cots as they slept. This was a different sort of motion. I slowly turned over and tried to look out from between the thin curtains that separated my sleeping corner from the rest of the room and saw the contours of a body moving quickly, as if it wanted to rove about unseen. I cautiously groped under the right side of my mattress and found my revolver. Even in my dream, I knew it was potentially lethal to sleep with an old, unreliable weapon under the mattress. Any day now, the movements of my body might disengage the safety and I would accidentally shoot myself or someone else just by sleeping restlessly. But I kept it there anyway. It made me feel like I was in control, and when I got hold of it beneath the thin mattress I slid slowly, slowly out of bed and onto the floor. The shadow moved again, now in a completely different part of the room, which was full of thin curtains. I moved toward the shadow slowly, keeping low. The curtains seemed to multiply the more I moved. The shadow was sometimes here, sometimes there, like a ghost out of the corner of my eye. The room seemed to have become infinitely huge, and I felt panic rising in my chest as I tried to shove all the cloth aside, but it was everywhere, blocking my way forward and backward. I lost my sense of direction. Suddenly I sensed movement right behind me. I turned around. The curtain behind me was hanging up in the air, a few meters away. I could see a pair of large boots sticking out under it. They were perfectly still. I raised my weapon. Aimed. I slowly reached out to move the cloth aside. Then, suddenly, it was pulled away from the other side. Standing before me was the skinny body of a boy in a pair of gigantic boots. His clothes were thin and ragged, even though it was the middle of winter. Snowflakes whirled around him. His head was a big red apple. I fired my weapon and the apple exploded.

⁂

I SAT UP so violently that I hit my head on the top bunk. Something was wrong. My body was wet and sticky, and the sheets smelled sour, as if someone had dumped a pail of water on me as I slept. I must have turned off my alarm in my sleep; it was later at night than I had expected. I hurtled out of bed and stumbled over to the monitors. By way of the grainy green screens I could see Jon moving nervously back and forth between the various surveillance cameras. He seemed to be running around the corridor and banging and yanking at doors as he shouted something. Suddenly he took off down the stairs and I hurried into the wall, shivering in my own cold sweat, to try to figure out what was going on. As he ran into the kitchen and I tried to follow, I heard whom he was looking for and what he was shouting. It was Franziska's name.

A FEW MINUTES later, the three of them who were left sat down in the kitchen. Henry made coffee—again—while Lotte tried to soothe Jon, who was on the verge of a breakdown. He alternately sat there with his head hanging between his legs like a person trying to overcome a dizzy spell, darted up to stare out the window, paced around the room, had an outburst, and sat down again. This went on for some time. Lotte, in her terry-cloth robe, gazed at him in concern as he paced and stroked his back gently when he sat down. Now and then she exchanged worried glances with Henry, who appeared to have aged since setting foot on the island a day and a half before. But I noticed that she observed Henry with at least as much concern even when he had his back to her. I assumed she had come to the conclusion that if there was no mysterious stranger hiding on the island, which seemed increasingly unlikely, then Henry was the top suspect. I was following Henry's movements in the kitchen when he suddenly looked right at the spot on the wall where I was hiding and stared directly at it. I was startled and quickly backed away from the peepholes. It occurred to me once again that the person, whoever it was, who had struck me when I found Katja must have inferred that I was still alive. Maybe that person was Henry. On the other hand, Lotte was the one who had brought a satellite phone to the island. Shadows seemed to be falling from every angle. Henry walked over to the table with the mugs of coffee, passed them around, and sat down. The two of them looked up at him as he said, "I think it's time for some straight talk."

HENRY

"SOMETHING IS GOING on here. Something we don't understand."

I had repeated this line several times in my head to make sure it would work as I intended. Lotte and Jon were still staring at me, and when no one said anything I went on: "Clearly someone or something here is causing people to disappear. We started out with seven of us. Now there are three of us. One is in a chest freezer half a floor down, and another is at the bottom of the sea. Two simply vanished. Is there anything either of you can tell me that might help us understand what happened?"

But still no one spoke. Lotte squirmed a little bit, but my hope that she would start talking was not fulfilled. So I kept going: "Then I'll start. I came here on a special assignment."

Lotte gasped sharply.

"Is there anything you'd like to say before I continue?"

She shook her head in silence, but her eyes shifted back and forth; she didn't want to meet my gaze. Instead her left hand flew to her mouth and she began to bite her nails, an absent expression on her face. I started talking again before she had time to gather her thoughts too much.

"I came here to watch over Anna Francis."

Lotte's eyes grew wide, but she still didn't say anything.

"That doesn't seem to have turned out so well, does it?" Jon sounded tired and angry. "What was the plan for watching over her, anyway? Get drunk, screw her, and fall asleep?"

He glared at me as if to say this whole situation was my fault.

"No, it didn't go so well. I didn't realize that we might be dealing with life-threatening situations; I understood it to mean that I was supposed to observe her."

"So why would Anna Francis be under observation?" Jon continued.

I looked at Lotte. She was still biting her nails and staring out the dark window. I tried to sound as if I were speaking straight from the heart, but in fact I was choosing my words carefully. Don't say too much; don't say too little.

"As I understood it, she was one of the most interesting candidates, but there was some uncertainty about how she would manage the pressure, so they wanted to keep an extra eye on her to see if she would break down."

Lotte looked doubtful.

"I don't get it. Why would they bring someone here if there was a risk she would have a breakdown?"

"I don't know much more than that. Apparently there are a number of things about her background that are unclear, but as far as I know they wanted to test her, in the hopes that she would manage well. I suppose she was just too good to pass up."

I could tell that Jon was trying to make sense of what I had just said.

"So, Henry . . ." he said slowly, "what does that make you? Are you even a candidate? Or are you just the secret police?"

"That," I said, "is something I'm not sure I have the right to tell you."

I went on before he could say more.

"I'm telling you this because you should know that I brought a gun with me to the island, due to this task; it's a service weapon I am permitted to possess because of my military rank and placement. And now that gun is missing."

"What the hell are you saying?" Jon said.

"My service weapon is gone. And I want to know if either of you took it. So now I have a question for you, and I really hope that you will answer it honestly. And before you respond, I want you to think about the fact that there is a loaded gun on this island and four people are already dead or missing. I don't think I need to remind you of the gravity of this situation." I allowed my gaze to wander between the two of them and tried to make eye contact with each. "Did either of you take my gun?"

Jon stared back at me with vacant eyes and shook his head slowly. I tried to get Lotte to look at me; at last she couldn't keep from meeting my gaze and speaking.

"No, I don't have your gun. But I also haven't been completely honest either. I *am* here as a candidate, but I had another assignment as well. I was supposed to observe the rest of you and then report back to the secretary and tell him how the events proceeded."

I latched on to this track right away.

"How were you supposed to do that?"

Lotte squirmed.

"I don't want to say."

"So you didn't bring a satellite phone with you?" I said.

She recoiled.

"How did you know?"

"You don't have to look so suspicious; Anna Francis and I saw you with it behind the house on the first night. You weren't particularly discreet about it."

Lotte looked pained.

"What *is* all this?" Jon exclaimed; apparently he had heard enough. "You've been sitting on a phone all this time? For God's sake, take it out and call for help! What are you waiting for?"

Lotte looked even unhappier.

"I don't have it anymore."

"What? Where the hell is it, then?"

"It was stolen. It disappeared the first day."

Jon heaved himself out of his chair and began to pace. Suddenly he stopped and stared hatefully at us.

"What the hell is wrong with all of you? You have a phone, you have a gun—you don't say a thing about them and now you've managed to lose every single useful object! *We are on a fucking island! There is nowhere to lose anything!*"

Neither of us said a word. His outburst seemed to have sapped the last of his strength, and he sat back down and looked dejectedly at Lotte. "A *phone*. Why didn't you say anything?"

"Maybe because I received strict orders from the start not to reveal the fact that I had a phone?"

Lotte sounded like she was about to start crying, the way you might near the end of a long, toxic fight.

"What were you really supposed to be keeping an eye on and reporting back about?" I asked.

She turned to me and squinted.

"Funny that you would be the one to ask."

"Why?"

"I was supposed to be keeping an eye on *you*."

This situation was slipping out of my hands like soap in a bathtub.

"Me?"

"Yes, you."

In an attempt to gain a little time and take back control, I quickly stood up and walked to the coffeemaker. With my back to the others, I picked up the carafe and slowly filled my cup as I tried to think fast.

"Why?" I said, my back still to the others.

There was a hint of schadenfreude in her voice.

"From what I heard, you were the wild card, the risky candidate."

I covered my eyes with my hand. This was too much to deal with. More than I'd expected. I cursed the secretary and all his mystery-making. It really would have been helpful to know all this.

Lotte went on; her voice began to sound hysterical.

"And now you're telling me that you've done some sort of mysterious service in the military and you brought a gun to the island, so tell me—why shouldn't I believe that *you* are the killer?"

I had truly lost control of the situation by now, and I had to recover it somehow. I took a step toward her, but she began to back up; her voice rose into a falsetto.

"Don't come any closer! It was you! Oh, my God, it was you! How could I be so stupid? How did I miss this? You were the one who was with Anna; you were the one who was in the boat with the colonel; it was you, you, you, you, you, *you goddamn murderer!*"

I took a quick step forward and slapped her face. In the shocked, dense silence that fell after the blow, I took her face between my hands and said, in as calm a voice as I could muster:

"I am not a murderer."

She stared back at me. Her eyes were wide and panicked, almost rolling back in her head. I held her eyes and said once more, softly and calmly, "I am not a murderer. You have to believe me."

Suddenly her body relaxed. She looked down.

"I'm sorry," she whispered. "I'm sorry. I'm just so scared."

I continued to hold her, more gently now. It was as if I were holding up her entire weight by supporting her head in my hands.

"You have every right to be scared. This is a tense situation; there is no such thing as a normal reaction to it. But if we're going to get out of here alive, we have to cooperate and stick together. We have to hold out until the boat arrives tomorrow afternoon, because right now it's our only hope."

"*If* it arrives."

That was Jon. His voice sounded broken.

"Who knows what's really going on here? Maybe they just gathered us all here in order to get rid of us. Who knows what the papers will say in a few days? Plane crash? Boating accident? Has that occurred to you two? What if they just want us to go away? Maybe there is no project after all."

I felt the hysteria spreading through the room again. Lotte's entire body began to tremble. I tried to take back control before it was too far gone.

"No matter what happens, we can't do anything right now. It's the middle of the night, it's still dark, and we wouldn't be able to find anyone now even if we try. My suggestion is that we go back to bed for a while longer, all of us. Either in our own rooms with the doors locked, or else we can all sleep in the same room. As soon as it gets light out we'll start searching the island again, for Franziska and the others. We're too tired and afraid right now. We need sleep and daylight to do anything more."

I looked from one to the other. Two pairs of tired, bloodshot eyes looked back at me. Jon gave a short nod. Lotte was still standing beside me, and I felt her arm against mine as she leaned against me. At least I seemed to have calmed her down enough that she no longer thought I was going to kill her.

"May I sleep in your room?" she asked in a small voice.

"Of course. How about you?" I turned to Jon. "There's plenty of room on the floor in my room."

He shook his head. "I'll take my own room."

"Lock the door."

"You don't have to tell me twice."

He rose from his chair and abruptly left the kitchen, his steps heavy. Lotte and I followed him up the stairs.

ANNA

As THEY WALKED up the stairs, I remained inside the kitchen wall and tried to master my breathing and my thoughts. Should I follow them up? Or should I go down to my basement and try to make sense of what I'd just heard? I couldn't quite get a grip on it. It felt like I was at a masquerade and all the guests had suddenly taken off their masks only to reveal new, grotesque ones underneath. Was Lotte tailing Henry? Was Henry tailing me? Or was it like Jon said, someone wanted to get rid of all of us? And if so, why? It seemed so absurd, but so did any explanation right now. Theories formed and burst as swiftly as soap bubbles. My breathing grew heavier and I felt like I was about to faint. Suddenly the walls seemed way too close, as if they were slowly pressing together over my chest. That familiar feeling of drowning from the inside, in your own body.

I realized that I had to get out of there before the panic attack struck full force, and on mincing steps I moved through the wall and down to the cellar, where I threw myself into the hallway and ended up on all fours, panting for breath. My head was spinning and my throat felt laced up tight, but the more air I tried to inhale, the more my head spun. My lips began to go numb and my hands felt like they were asleep. I knew what was happening, but I couldn't hold it back any longer.

I lay on the floor in a fetal position and tried to follow the lines of the oblong baseboard with my eyes, just as I had learned. "Breathe in rectangles," said the self-help book someone had lent me when the panic attacks were at their worst in Kyzyl Kum. That helped sometimes, but this time it was too late for that sort of trick. Lying on my side made me feel nauseated; I tried to turn onto my stomach, but that was even worse. It was like every part of my body, every organ, every single cell, needed to vomit. I tried to sit up, but my head was spinning too fast and I ended up lying on my back with my legs tucked up as I rubbed my face with my hands, as if I were trying to make sure it wouldn't disappear.

The yellow light in the basement cavern made the room seem even smaller and very close, and I tried and failed to ignore the thought that I was running out of oxygen. That was the worst part about panic-attack thinking, that as soon as you had a thought, it was as if it became true, no matter how inconceivable and unrealistic it was. My heart was pounding like a dormouse's. The ceiling sank lower and lower; I breathed harder and harder; black spots began to appear in my vision. I curled up in a fetal position again and tried to focus on the wall clock; the minutes passed, ten minutes, fifteen minutes, thirty minutes. The panic came and went in waves, but it didn't ease up.

And then I thought of the bottle of pills I had grabbed earlier up in the medical station. Or had that thought been there all along? Had I just been waiting for the right moment to open the bottle? The perfect excuse.

WHEN I CAME home from Kyzyl Kum, I was addicted to FLL. At least that's what the doctors said. I wasn't so sure, myself. It was actually one of the field doctors who gave me FLL for the first time, after I complained of difficulty concentrating. Because the more chaotic the situation in Kyzyl Kum became, the harder I found it to do one thing at a time. My headaches from the explosions would hang around for weeks. It was like there was always this rushing sound in my head, louder and louder. The doctor who gave me the FLL explained that it was an experimental drug for people with diagnoses that involved serious concentration problems. He also explained that it was relatively untested, and despite the fact that most of those who had tried it reported a positive experience, not much was known about the long-term effects. But the nasty thing about FLL wasn't that it lacked sufficient clinical trials to be used in the well-established health care system back home; the scary part was that it worked so well. Instead of whirling around like one big mess in my head, my entire existence suddenly dropped down into various boxes, all perfectly organized and sorted. Suddenly I was able to work with great concentration until I was actually finished with something, even if everything around me was chaos.

At first I took my pills only when things were extra stressful. It didn't seem all that remarkable. Other people drank; I didn't. Although I had self-medicated with alcohol on occasion earlier in my life, I didn't dare do so then, because I became far too clumsy and hungover, and I experienced excessive anxiety. Plus it made my headaches worse. FLL didn't have those effects at all. In fact, I enjoyed that membrane that would drop down between me and reality. It made things sortable and kept them at a comfortable distance; it made me feel calmer and more focused instead of troubled by constantly spinning, troublesome thoughts. In time it seemed silly, almost irresponsible, not to take the pills more often, because they helped me function better. Other people needed me to function. I began to take the tablets almost daily. And yet it never felt like a habit. I had no problems abstaining on a quiet day.

In time, it became clear that there were downsides. I couldn't sleep. Instead of relaxing, I lay there wide awake, staring at the ceiling and trying to sort out my life in my thousand tiny inner boxes. I became increasingly exhausted, and I started taking sleeping pills so I could wind down. Somewhere around that point was where it all began to go off the rails. My thoughts became more and more muddled, and my hands started to shake. So I took more pills to get rid of the tremors. At the same time, the situation in the region escalated and became more dangerous, both inside and outside the camp. I constantly ran into conflict with the military arm of the effort, the people who really just wanted to bomb the whole region to pieces. People began to avoid me. I started making mistakes. Forgivable ones at first, and, later, unforgivable ones.

When I was finally sent home and admitted to the hospital, they said it was for addiction and rehabilitation. I surrendered myself to care, but in secret I never truly believed that FLL was my problem. For me, it wasn't really all that difficult to stop taking the pills, especially when they threatened to take Siri away from me permanently if I didn't go through "the Comrades' Twelve Steps to Sobriety." The rehab center I was eventually moved to was perhaps the most depressing place I had ever been, including the refugee camp in Kyzyl Kum. We had group therapy sessions, in which miners from Kiruna with large port-wine noses cried about how they had drunk away the family Volvo, and young party members sobbed over how they had missed out on top jobs due to imported cocaine.

I lied at those meetings. I lied as I had never lied before. I played the most brilliant role of my life, crying and shaking, alternately denying my problems and having revelations, and I received standing ovations as thanks for my efforts. No one saw through me. Or else they all saw through me, but weren't actually all that interested. It didn't matter to me; I lied my way through treatment and out of the rehab center, back to my own apartment and my old job. I left the rehab center in October, on a day when the daylight didn't even try. I stood in the circle and everyone got to say their final words to me. We hugged and exchanged the obligatory contact information. When I got home to my apartment, I threw all those slips of paper into the trash and immediately took the bag to the garbage chute, where it vanished with that tumbling suction rumble that sounded like you had just opened a portal straight out into space.

Then it was back to everyday life, that utterly colorless time. I was back at my job, but I soon asked to be given less demanding tasks, using my condition as an excuse. You could

say that I basically just sorted paper clips. Day in and day out.
My coworkers tried to pretend that everything was normal,
but I noticed them watching me and avoiding me, the way you
make a wide berth around a car accident but at the same time
you can't help but stare. Sometimes, when newspapers wanted
to interview me or when they called from TV news programs
and invited me to comment on the situation in Kyzyl Kum, I
hung up on them. Sometimes I wrote e-mails and pretended
to be my own secretary, who informed them that I needed
peace and quiet for reasons that were slightly unclear. Sometimes I wrote that I was, unfortunately, out of town. It didn't
matter to me if they knew I was bluffing. I went straight home
after work and spent the nights alone in my apartment. Sometimes I thought about Henry. It was winter, and it was dark
around the clock.

On weekends and on Wednesday nights, I went to visit Siri
and Nour. I tried to find an excuse to cancel every time, even
though I constantly longed for Siri. I always went. We never
quite had the discussion about when Siri would move back.
Sometimes I discovered Nour studying me when she thought
I wasn't looking. I also noticed that she was unwilling to leave
me alone with Siri for any length of time. Apparently I hadn't
fooled her.

I CRAWLED OVER to my clothes, dug the pill bottle out of my
pocket, and poured a whole pile of tablets into my palm. They
felt so familiar in my hand, like something that should have
been there long ago, that always should have been there. Pale
blue and round against my skin. They had cost me so much;

the doctors and therapists at the rehab center would surely have said that they almost ruined my life. I pushed those thoughts aside and popped the pills into my mouth. I swallowed hard and waited for the panic to subside, the way it usually did. That release, like a tide going out, like a storm rolling away. I lay down on my side again, waiting, breathing. And then, slowly, I felt the panic sink back, but it still wasn't quite how I had imagined. My head felt odd, light, as if it were a balloon. I couldn't quite orient myself in the room. It struck me that I probably didn't have the same tolerance I'd had before, when I was taking them every day, sometimes several times a day. I had just swallowed a handful of pills, and I didn't really know how they would affect me. But in any case, it was better. Everything was better than it had been a minute ago.

I lay on my back and let my head float around just as it wanted to. My breathing started to return to normal. My eyes roved over the ceiling. That was when I saw it. Deep in one corner. A small but unmistakable black eye. A camera. I stood up, unsteadily, and walked over to it. It was too high for me to reach, so I awkwardly dragged a chair over and climbed onto it, my legs trembling. It really did look like the eye of a camera. I waved my hand in front of it, the way kids do when they see themselves on a security cam in a store. It was impossible to tell whether it was on.

I climbed back down off the chair and looked around the room. On the other side was a three-legged stool made of metal. I grabbed it, climbed up on the chair again, and slammed the stool into the wall with all my strength, right next to the camera. It left a small mark, but nothing more. I flipped the stool around and tried using its legs instead. That worked better. The wall gave a crunch, and after a few more bangs I managed to knock a hole in the wall. I stuck my hand in and was able to pry the camera out a little bit. It was attached to the wall with cords. A tiny blue light glowed on the part of the camera that had been hidden behind the wall. Apparently it was on. Even in my condition, I knew what that meant. Someone was watching me.

All of a sudden, I had had enough of all this. It was a very hasty decision. I took hold of the camera and yanked it with all my might, and it came loose from the wall. A tangle of cords followed it, like guts attached to a larger organ. The blue light faded and slowly went out. I placed the camera on the floor, grabbed the metal stool, and aimed a blow. On the first attempt, the stool struck the floor a few inches from the camera; on the second, I hit my mark. A piece of black plastic flew off. The lens was the next piece to bite the dust, and a few shards of glass hit the floor. It occurred to me that if anyone was watching me right now, they knew that I had found the camera—but it didn't matter, because I had already decided I didn't care. When I was done, I fumblingly put on my clothes, tucked the gun into my waistband at the small of my back, and climbed up through the hatch.

I lay in the chest freezer for a while, the code coming and going in my memory, but at last I managed to unlock the lid. I went through the medical station and out into the hall. It was perfectly quiet in the house, as if it were truly asleep. Not just the people inside it, but the house itself. I opened the front door. It felt like when I was a teenager and tried to sneak home drunk without attracting Nour's attention, only this time I was sneaking out. Once I walked through the door, I realized how cold it was. The wind was no longer blowing at hurricane strength, but it was still a cold and forbidding wind. It was an unbearable temperature for a person wearing only jeans and a camisole, but the cold couldn't touch me. This was the first time I had been outdoors, and visible, in two days, and it felt odd, like I was changing clothes in a public square.

I stood on the lawn outside the house, barefoot in the half-light, looking out over the sea. It was truly empty in all directions. There was nowhere to go, no door to bang on, no emergency number to call. It was starting to feel like I was back in the camp at Kyzyl Kum. Maybe I had never left.

As my feet slowly went numb from the cold, I stood there and calmly tried to think of what I should do next. It occurred to me that I should try to talk to Jon. Whatever was happening on this island, I had the impression that he was not involved. If he was, he was a much better actor than I could have suspected. Everything he had shown since I vanished suggested that he was honestly confused and upset about what was going on. I turned around and went back into the house, trying to plan how I might try to explain to him that I wasn't dead, but then I realized that he would, of course, see that for himself and I decided that I probably wouldn't need to give an explanation.

I SNEAKED UP the grand staircase as quietly and discreetly as I could, letting my hand run along the extravagant wood carvings, and once I reached the hallway I took a left, away from the wing where Henry and Lotte's rooms were. I walked up to the thick wooden door of Jon's room, took a breath, and knocked.

No response. I didn't dare knock again, as it was far too loud, so instead I tested the door handle. The door wasn't locked. I cracked it and peered into the room; then I allowed the door to open all the way. It gave a slight creak and remained ajar. The bed was unmade and clothes were strewn everywhere. But aside from that, the room was empty. I took a few steps in. The bathroom door was wide open, and no one was in there either. A black leather toiletry bag was balancing on the edge of the sink and there were a few hand towels on the floor. The toilet lid and seat were both up. But there was no Jon in sight.

I HEARD A sound but couldn't tell where it was coming from. My hand went to the gun at my waistband, and I pulled it out. It felt cold and heavy. I cautiously sneaked back into the hallway. The door of Henry's room was ajar. I felt faint and my heart was pounding; something was making my eyes sticky, and I soon realized that it was perspiration trickling into them from my forehead. My whole body was in a cold sweat. I walked toward Henry's room and tried to peer in. Lotte was in the bed, tucked under the blanket.

"Lotte! Lotte!"

I tried to whisper, but I wasn't sure whether the words actually came out. No reaction. I took a few steps toward the bed. She was lying with her back to me, and a little bit of her terry-cloth robe stuck out at the edge of the blanket. I touched her shoulder. No reaction. I shook her a little harder, and she almost melted onto her back, lifeless. I screamed her name and shook her hard, but nothing happened. My heart was pounding in my ears; it sounded like I was standing next to a freight train. I tried to think, but it felt like I didn't really need to anymore. There was only one answer left for all these questions, one single answer. I heard a sound behind me and turned around, the revolver curiously heavy in my hand.

IN THE DOORWAY stood Henry. My hands trembled as I aimed the weapon at him, and I had to hold it with both hands. We stared at each other. Neither of us said anything for a few seconds.

"So it was you," I said at last. My voice sounded strange in my ears.

"Yes, it was me," Henry said at last, in a low voice. "But it's not what you think. Put down the gun so I can explain."

He took a half step forward. I flipped off the safety.

"Don't come any closer. Don't you fucking come any closer to me."

Henry didn't move.

"Anna," he said in a voice that was low and full of concentration. "Put down the gun. I can explain. You're not yourself right now. What did you take?"

He took another half step forward.

"Don't come any closer!" I shouted. Sweat was running into my eyes; my body felt cold and sticky. The gun seemed absurdly heavy in my hands, and my arms were trembling visibly by now. I forced the words out: "Personal dossiers on me and guns in secret cabinets! One person vanishing after the next! You knew, you knew all along. You were the one who knocked me out in the medical station, weren't you?"

"Yes, that was me."

"You were the one who made the others disappear, weren't you?"

"Yes, that was me, but listen, please, Anna, *it's not what you think*. If you'll just put down the gun . . ."

He lunged suddenly, a few quick steps toward me, his arm reaching for the weapon. I closed my eyes and fired.

Henry bounced backward, all the way to the wall, and collapsed. A trickle of blood ran down his forehead. The wall behind him was completely spattered in red. There was something white, sort of like oatmeal, on the floor. His body gave a few jerks and he slithered down a little farther, until he was half reclining, a doll that had been tossed into a corner. I dropped the gun right on the floor and left the room, walked out into the hallway, down the stairs, and out the door.

It looked like it was going to be a beautiful day. The wind had died down and the layer of clouds was beginning to break up. A few rays of the rising sun found their way to the lawn, which was glowing a surreal silvery gray. I walked barefoot on the grass alongside the path and down to the ladder at the edge of the cliff. Seabirds were diving at the water and the glittering sun danced across the rippling sea, as if schools of golden fish were swimming just below the surface. I dangled my feet over the cliff edge and noticed that flecks of blood came pretty high up my pant legs. Far below, I saw the white foam of the waves washing over rocks and tufts of seaweed at the water's edge. The waves rolled in again and again, like a perpetual motion machine. I gazed out across the sea. Far off on the horizon, I saw an approaching helicopter. First one, then two.

STOCKHOLM

THE PROTECTORATE OF SWEDEN

MAY 2037

THE COLONEL

COLONEL PER OLOF Ehnmark was sitting across from them now. He looked a wreck. His eyes were red and his body seemed to hang on his skeleton like a heavy blanket draped over a delicate branch. It looked like he could barely manage to hold himself up. Around him hovered the faint but unmistakable scent of old booze. He didn't look like he cared.

He, the lead interrogator, was the one to start. They had made this decision together. Old military men often preferred to speak to other men. He reached for the tape recorder, pressed the button, and leaned toward it a bit as if he didn't quite trust its ability to capture the sound in the room.

"The tape is rolling. Initial interrogation of Colonel Ehnmark. I'd first like to thank you for taking the time to assist us."

"I don't suppose I had much of a choice." The colonel's voice sounded as tired as his body looked.

"You are free to leave whenever you like, naturally." She was the one to interject.

"Well, isn't that generous of you," said the colonel. Then he didn't say anything further. Apparently he wasn't planning to make this easy for them. Silence ruled for a moment, until she nudged him discreetly in the side. They had to begin.

"Well?" he said encouragingly to the colonel.

"Well?"

"Colonel, I need a confirmation from you. Are you participating in this interrogation of your own free will?"

If it was possible, the colonel looked even more tired.

"Do we really have to go through that procedure? Yes . . ."

"I'm sorry?"

"Yes, I am participating in this interrogation involving the incidents on Isola of my own free will. Because I assume that's what you want to talk about?"

The lead interrogator squirmed with a twinge of awkwardness.

"I apologize, but . . ."

"No, right, I am the only one who has to give out any information here, of course. Yes, I am participating voluntarily. Can we get on with it now?"

Both his shoulders and hers relaxed a fraction of an inch, and he began the interrogation.

"Naturally. Okay, I would like to begin by asking when you found out that Anna Francis was the mark."

"The mark?"

"The true candidate."

The colonel appeared to be thinking back. It was impossible to tell if he truly needed to consider his answer or if he was just trying to annoy them by taking his time.

"I suspected it from the start. From what I understood of

the project, she had the perfect profile. What's more, I had heard rumors that there might be . . ."

The colonel cut himself off. The chief interrogator urged him on.

"Yes?"

"Well, what to call it? The potential for coercion?"

"Could you be more specific?"

"I don't know; I suppose these were more or less just rumors I had heard."

"What did those rumors say?"

The colonel looked uncomfortable and shifted in his chair.

"That she failed somehow toward the end of her time in Kyzyl Kum. That there had been some trouble."

"What kind of trouble?"

The colonel shrugged.

"I don't know, the usual? PTSD, drugs, breakdowns, some reckless decisions? The same things that afflict everyone sooner or later, everyone who does that sort of work. Same old story, like I said."

"You were stationed in that region yourself for a considerable period of time, weren't you?"

The question was posed in a mild tone, but the colonel seemed to pinpoint the underlying threat immediately.

"Yes, and I'm absolutely certain the two of you have read my file and everything worth knowing inside it, but if this conversation turns to *my* old, bad decisions for even one second, it's over, so you might as well stop trying that tactic on me. I'm sure you could make my life hell in many ways, but I'm too old to care. I've already lost most of what meant anything to me, and if I'm not mistaken, *you* are the ones who want to talk to *me* right now. Do you understand the difference? You want something from me, and if you so much as hint that you want to mess with me I will stand up and walk out of here."

"I apologize, Colonel."

The lead interrogator looked chagrined.

"I accept your apology," the colonel said, but he didn't appear to mean it.

The lead interrogator nudged the second interrogator in the side as if to signal that she should take over, but she remained silent. It wasn't time yet. So he went on.

"You say that you'd heard the 'same old story' about Anna Francis. Had you heard anything that could not be described as the 'same old story'?"

"Well, that would be the bit about . . ." He was hesitant.

"Go on."

"I suppose that would be the bit about the boy."

"The bit about the boy?"

"That she had shot that boy. That that's what broke her."

"Can you expand on that?"

The colonel gave a deep sigh as if he were utterly tired of them and their clumsy tactics.

"No, as a matter of fact I can't, and given that I'm sure you know more than I do about these incidents, I find it absolutely unnecessary for me to sit here and speculate."

The lead interrogator cast a glance down at his papers, but in reality he was looking at her hands. She was making a little circle sign with her index finger, as if to tell him he should continue. They had their little signals. A slight lift of the index finger meant *my turn*; pointed forward it meant *Keep inquiring about this.* Now it was time to move on, to avoid getting him worked up in vain. Besides, they'd gotten what they wanted here.

"Okay. We'll leave it at that. You say that you suspected from the start that she was the candidate they were interested in. Did that change?"

"It changed when she disappeared, of course. Or died. Or however I should put it."

"You were convinced that she was dead when it happened?"

"Yes, I was with the doctor . . . Katja, who found her. Did you drug me? I assume you did."

He lifted his gaze from the tabletop and allowed his red-rimmed eyes to move between the two of them. She moved her index finger back and forth: *Don't answer.*

"I apologize, Colonel, I don't have the authority to release any details about the operation."

The colonel chuckled, a laugh devoid of pleasure.

"Of course you drugged me. I suppose Anna herself did it. During dinner, I presume? Well done; I didn't notice a thing. You certainly selected a suitable candidate. Smart of you to let me see her dead body as well. I definitely would have become suspicious otherwise."

"Had you met Anna Francis before you encountered her on Isola?"

"No, and I'm sure you were already aware of that fact too. That was the first time I had met her."

"What was your impression of her?"

The colonel leaned back a shade and didn't say anything for a long time. When he did answer, he appeared to be choosing his words carefully.

"She seemed tense. It was obvious that she had been living under extreme pressure. Even if I hadn't known anything about her, I would have suspected that she had experienced war; she had that look around the eyes that people get."

"What do you mean?"

"It's hard to put my finger on it. But it does something to you. I could see that she was watchful. She never turned her back to the room; she never left herself open to attack. I'm the same way, so I recognize the behavior. You get that way once you've had to watch your own back in earnest."

"Would you describe her as stable?"

"Yes, I think so. She wasn't nuts, or neurotic, if that's what you mean. She gave the impression of being levelheaded and in control. But she was on guard."

"How would you describe her relationship with Henry Fall?"

"I couldn't quite make sense of it. On the one hand, they acted as if they didn't know each other; on the other hand, I had the impression that they actually did. It seemed as if she were extra vigilant toward him, and for that matter he was vigilant toward her too. When she disappeared, my theory was that he might be the candidate. That would have explained her vigilance. But then it occurred to me that there could have been another reason for it."

"What might that have been?"

The colonel looked amused and once again let his gaze move from him to her and back to him again.

"Surely not even someone like you could be so ruined by power games and tactics that you can't think of a reason for a man and a woman to pay extra attention to each other."

"Oh, that's what you mean. I see," said the lead interrogator.

The colonel responded to him but looked at her, an amused glint in his eyes:

"Are you totally sure of that?"

"I'm sorry?" The lead interrogator sounded offended.

She was thinking that she would soon have to take over, since the colonel was on the verge of gaining an advantage. He was guiding this interrogation now. When he entered the room, she'd found it difficult to match this broken man across from them with the efficient one she had read about in the reports from Isola, but now she was beginning to see a hint of him.

The lead interrogator tried a fresh start.

"Did you ever suspect that she wasn't dead?"

"Not at first, but when Katerina Ivanovitch disappeared too, of course I started to wonder. It was really too good to be true."

"Too good?"

"You know what I mean. People don't just start vanishing left and right when it comes to this sort of exercise. I've been around long enough to know that."

The lead interrogator paged through his documents.

"Let's go back to the moment when Anna Francis disappeared. How did the others react?"

"With alarm, I would say."

"Was there any reaction that stood out in particular?"

"Well, Fall certainly seemed extremely shaken."

"Would you say that anyone was overly shaken?"

The colonel seemed to understand what he was getting at.

"If you're wondering if one of the others became suspicious then and there, the answer is no. He was very clever about it. And that love story was a good cover, of course. Was it planned?"

"Unfortunately I am unable . . ."

The colonel gave an audible sigh.

"You can't give any details, yes, I know. It was a smart idea, in any case, whoever it was that thought of it."

Now it was her turn. She wanted to change the subject, preferably without arousing the colonel's suspicions.

"Let's move on. What happened then?"

"We decided to search the island."

"Who took the initiative in doing so?"

"I don't remember."

She leaned back and continued to watch him. Tried to keep her tone mild.

"Others we spoke to say that you took the initiative."

"That could be. But it could have been anyone; it was the natural thing to do."

She went on:

"I would like to jump forward in time. Now I want to hear about what happened when you received instructions from Henry Fall that you were to disappear."

The colonel grew silent for a moment and appeared to be searching his memory. For the first time, his answer was hesitant.

"It started when someone called out that the pier had come loose, and in hindsight I guess I have to assume Henry Fall loosened it when he was part of the group that was searching around the boathouse area."

"So what did you do then?"

"We ran down to the bottom of the cliff and put in the

boat. Fall made sure that he and I were the only ones who went out. Von Post wanted to come along, as I recall, but Fall said no."

"So the two of you went out in the boat . . ."

"And that was where I received my instructions."

"What were they?"

"He informed me that the operation was all about Anna Francis, just as I had suspected earlier. That she wasn't dead but thought she was the one observing us, and that the stress test involved all of us disappearing one after the next. They were planning to reassure themselves that she could handle the pressure and continue to obey orders. To put it simply, that she wouldn't break down."

"What sort of technical instructions did you receive?"

"I was supposed to place the oxygen regulator in my mouth, overturn the boat, and wait underneath it, and once the others went back up to the house I would flip the boat again, drive it around the island, and join Katerina Ivanovitch at the gathering place on the other side."

She searched through her papers, found a map of the island, and placed it in the middle of the table.

"Can you show me how you got around?"

The colonel bent over the table and studied the map, showing with one finger how he had made his way halfway around the island and landed at a very small, narrow inlet off the northeastern corner of the house, a point that could hardly have been visible from the house since it was directly under the gable. To get there by land, one had to go through the thick brambles on the steep rise.

"I walked up here, and here's where I got in."

"You mean into the underground shelter?"

"Yes, on the back side of the island, under the house."

"Was it difficult to get to the gathering place without being spotted?"

"No, it wasn't a problem. Everyone else was busy in the house, and Katja was already in the shelter, of course."

"What about the boat? Wasn't there a risk that someone would notice it eventually?"

The colonel looked tired.

"As you may recall, it was inflatable. I deflated it and brought it in with me."

"So I should interpret this to mean that as long as you were actively taking part in it, the operation functioned smoothly."

"Yes, I would say so. Inhumane though it was."

The lead interrogator broke in again. She cast an irritated glance at him. This was not how they had planned the interrogation. She didn't appreciate his deviating from the protocol.

"What impression did you get from the others when they joined you? Did it still seem to be functioning smoothly?"

"I got that impression, yes."

"No one mentioned any uncertainties regarding Henry Fall's actions?"

"What kind of uncertainties do you mean?"

"I'm asking you."

"It's hard to respond when I don't understand the question."

Now they were both leaning over the table.

The lead investigator pressed on: "Was there any reason to believe that Fall was losing control of the operation?"

She wanted to stop him. She tried to signal him with her finger, tell him not to go any further, but it was too late.

"I don't understand what you're trying to get at. Why don't you ask Fall directly?"

The lead interrogator realized too late that he had guided the conversation down the wrong path. He leaned back and tried to adopt a dismissive expression.

"Unfortunately I am barred from . . ."

The colonel looked increasingly puzzled.

"Did something happen? Did something go wrong?"

"Colonel . . ."

"Did something happen to Anna? Is she dead?"

"Anna Francis is alive, Colonel."

She kicked the lead interrogator hard under the table. She needed to intervene, but she didn't quite know how. The colonel was bent over the table, and by now it was more like he was interrogating the lead interrogator.

"So the problem is with Fall. What happened? Did he reveal his role?"

The lead interrogator threw up his hands in desperation.

"I'm sorry, but I am unable to . . ."

The colonel stood up and leaned across the table. His face was close to the lead interrogator; he was almost shouting.

"Answer me now, or I will ask him myself!"

"Unfortunately, I must inform you that that would be impossible. Henry Fall is dead."

The colonel just stared at him. The second interrogator had to fight the urge to bury her face in her hands.

"Dead? What the hell . . ."

"I apologize, Colonel, I thought you knew," she said quietly, although she knew that wasn't true. That it would have been preferable if he never found out, had it been possible to avoid telling him. The colonel looked from one to the other, his eyes wild.

"For God's sake. Oh, God . . . what have you done?"

She bent toward the tape recorder and said curtly:

"Interrogation concluded 12:36."

She turned it off. The colonel grabbed his jacket, which he had hung on the back of his chair. She could see that his hands were shaking. Without a glance at either of them, he left the room.

KATJA

KATJA MET THE colonel in the corridor. He was walking fast, his head down, and he almost ran into her. She was just about to say hello as he looked up, but she stopped when she saw the expression on his face. He bent down to her.

"Were you in on this mess?"

He nearly spat the words; the guard behind him came up and took hold of him.

"Colonel, I apologize, but the witnesses are not allowed to speak to each other."

He stared hard at her, but she said nothing. He shook off the guard's hand.

"God damn it," he said, staring hatefully at her; then he made his way through the corridor with long strides. She swallowed and continued down the corridor, to the door that led into the interrogation room.

"AT WHAT STAGE did you join the operation?"

The man was asking. The woman sat quietly, brandishing

a pen, clearly ready to take notes. She held her notepad at an angle, so Katja couldn't tell whether she was writing yet. She wondered if this was a tactic to make her feel insecure.

"I came in once they had settled on Anna Francis."

"What do you know about how that decision was reached?"

"I understand there were other potential candidates, but they had chosen to bet on her."

The lead interrogator looked down at his papers and gave a hum.

"What did you know about Anna's background?"

Just answer the questions, Katja thought. *Not too much and not too little. Just answer the questions.*

"I knew of her, but so did everyone, more or less."

"How did you know of her?"

"Well, from magazines, TV . . . her work in Kyzyl Kum."

"But you knew more about her than what was written in the magazines, didn't you?"

This was the woman, the second interrogator, speaking. She smiled. There was an intimacy and directness in the way she spoke. As if they were only confirming what they already knew. Katja's answer was hesitant.

"Well, I did have access to the report on her time in Kyzyl Kum."

"What did it say?"

"It . . . it doesn't feel quite right to discuss that here. You know, some of this is . . ."

"Classified?" The second interrogator was still smiling her courteous little smile.

"I don't know if I am supposed to answer that question."

The second interrogator leaned over to the tape recorder on the table and said, "Pausing the tape."

ONCE THE TAPE was rolling again, the second interrogator was once more the one to start off:

"Katerina Ivanovitch has been shown the documents in which the Chairman authorizes both her and myself to discuss the material found in the classified report SOR 234:397 Class 3. I will ask again: What information was in the documents you were shown before you traveled to the island?"

"Well, there was quite a bit there. She suffered from PTSD, of course . . ."

"Post-traumatic stress disorder."

"Yes, exactly, and as I understood it she had also had some problems with her use of FLL."

The second interrogator looked at her with interest, one eyebrow raised.

"You say 'use.' Not 'abuse'?"

Katja shifted in her chair. She had known that this would come up, and she felt relatively well prepared.

"It's hard to tell. She had lived under extreme circumstances for quite a long time. I would say that it is not abnormal to self-medicate with narcotics or anti-anxiety medications, or to develop PTSD under those circumstances. In fact, those things would suggest a functional person. It *would* be abnormal not to allow oneself to be affected by those circumstances."

"I understand," said the second interrogator, even as she appeared not to want to or be able to understand. "Was that why you eventually accepted that FLL should be made accessible to her on the island?"

"Well, no . . . No. I didn't think that was a good idea."

"You even went so far as to submit a written protest—why?"

The question was posed in that same mild tone, but a hint of harshness had slipped into her voice.

"I thought it was unnecessarily cruel. Someone who has managed to stop using shouldn't be exposed to the risk of falling back into it. Not under such pressing circumstances."

The second interrogator tilted her head as if she didn't quite understand.

"And yet you don't want to label her an abuser? Not even in light of what has happened?"

"No, I think that word is too strong. It's misleading."

"Did you know that she had undergone treatment for her abuse?"

"Yes, I did, and I knew that it was successful."

"Who told you that?"

"Secretary Nordquist. And it was evident in the report, as well."

The second interrogator jotted down another note and then went on.

"What made you eventually accept that FLL would be planted in the medical room?"

"The secretary explained how incredibly important it was for us to find out whether she was sufficiently rehabilitated not to have a relapse of ab . . . of use, no matter how pressing the situation. He felt that we couldn't afford to bet on the wrong horse when it came to this job."

The second interrogator looked up from her papers.

"Were those his words? 'Bet on the wrong horse'?"

"As I recall, yes."

The second interrogator continued to take notes. Katja wondered what she was writing.

"So in the end, you went along with placing FLL on the island, like a sort of test of character?"

"Yes. Wasn't the whole thing a sort of test of character?" Katja said, immediately regretting her words.

THE SECRETARY

"WHOSE IDEA WAS it to place FLL on the island?"

This was the woman, the second interrogator, speaking. He would have preferred to speak with the lead interrogator. It was always easier to talk to men. Maybe they knew he felt this way; maybe that was why they were letting her handle his interrogation. He decided not to let it affect him. But he had absolutely no desire to talk to a nagging bitch in uniform.

"What do you mean, 'whose idea'?"

"I mean just that. Whose idea was it to place FLL on Isola?"

"I'd have to go back and look through my notes if you want an answer to that. I don't remember offhand."

She gave him a disarming smile, as if this was exactly what she had hoped he would say.

"That's no problem! We have all the background material right here. We can take a short break so you can check."

The secretary shook his head. *Shit.*

"No, it would take too long to find it. I don't even recall where that note might be."

Her smile grew even wider. He thought she looked like a snake about to swallow her prey whole.

"We can take a break. So you have time to look up what you need to know to answer these questions. After all, they're your own meeting minutes, so I'm sure it won't take *that* long. Besides, we have all the time in the world. So . . ." She looked at her colleague, who gave a brief nod.

"Okay, pausing the tape at 16:49 . . ."

The secretary shook his head and waved his hand.

"No, no . . . that won't be necessary. We can continue."

She looked at him, her head at an angle, and appeared to arrive at a decision.

"Then I will ask the question for a third time: Whose idea was it?"

He had to say something. He cleared his throat.

"There was a meeting that included a discussion of which weaknesses we needed to test our candidate for. And this came up as a particular worry, that there had been a history of addiction. It was important to find out how serious it was. And then someone suggested we could make the drug available and see if she would misappropriate it in a high-stress situation."

She persisted.

"So it was your idea?"

"I don't remember whose idea it was."

With the same amused smile she had kept on her lips all along, she picked up a few sheets of paper in front of her, appeared to find what she was looking for, flipped to the correct page, and began to read out loud.

"'The secretary therefore suggests that we should make FLL accessible on the island to see if AF will suffer a relapse of

abuse during an extremely stressful situation.' Meeting minutes from the sixteenth of January. Is this familiar to you?"

"Like I said, it was a discussion," the secretary said acidly.
"I don't remember if it was me or someone else who came up
with the suggestion."

"Is there any reason to doubt the accuracy of the minutes?"

He muttered something under his breath. She continued
to stare at him with those goddamn well-groomed eyebrows
raised high on her forehead. He looked at her colleague, but
he appeared to be thinking about something else, his eyes
drifting far beyond the secretary's head. Apparently there was
no help to be found there.

"Please answer the question."

She wouldn't give up.

"No. There isn't," the secretary responded curtly.

The lead interrogator appeared to wake from his trance.
He began to sift through the documents before him. The
second interrogator bent over and whispered something to
him, and he gave a short nod before speaking. "I'd like to talk
a bit about the selection of Anna Francis. Isn't it true that you
were against her as a candidate? That the Chairman was the
one who wanted her?"

"It's true that the Chairman suggested her."

"Were you of a different opinion?"

"There were other candidates with other qualities."

"And what did you see as Anna Francis's weaknesses?"

"In an organization like the RAN group, it is important for
people to be goal oriented. Pragmatic. To see the bigger picture."

The secretary felt like he was on safer ground here. He

could hear it in his own voice. It sounded more like normal, more confident.

"And that wasn't true of Anna Francis?"

Now it was back to the bitch with the eyebrows. The secretary pretended she wasn't there; instead he continued to look at the lead interrogator as he answered.

"Let's just say that she'd had certain problems with those things earlier."

"What are you referring to?"

She wouldn't give up.

"This Socratic method you're using is rather annoying," the secretary snapped. "Can't you just ask me what you want to know?"

She was still smiling. He wished she would wipe off that goddamn sneering smile.

"I'd be glad to, if you'd go into a little more detail," she said, then continued: "What did you have against Anna Francis?"

"She was too obsessed with ethics."

The second interrogator's eyebrows went up even farther, if that was possible.

"Goodness, isn't that an unusual objection? Too obsessed with ethics? You don't believe that ethics are useful in the RAN group?"

"There's a difference between being ethical and having a Jesus complex. Sometimes you have to make tough decisions and it's no use getting sentimental." He shot the lead interrogator a pleading look, since he had gotten the impression that the man understood him better. But the man said nothing; he allowed his colleague to continue.

"And did she?"

"Well, it was pretty obvious that she took far too sentimental an outlook during certain sensitive situations in Kyzyl Kum, wasn't it?"

"Which situations are you referring to?"

The secretary was suddenly tired of this whole situation.

"For Christ's sake, don't just sit there grinning and pretend you don't know what happened when she stopped obeying orders."

He immediately regretted his outburst when he saw the second interrogator's smile broaden further.

"I do know what happened, but I'm mostly curious about what you consider examples of her excessive sentimentality."

The secretary sat quietly and didn't respond. He found it disturbing that she had caused him to lose his footing. The lead interrogator took the floor again.

"Wasn't it the case that the catastrophe itself occurred because no one listened to her?"

The secretary gave a deep sigh.

"No, that is not my understanding. She was the problem. A civilian aid worker in the field is not supposed to be in charge. She is supposed to obey her military superiors."

"Even if they're wrong?"

The secretary crossed his arms over his chest and said nothing. The first interrogator looked down at his papers again before he went on:

"So it sounds like you were never that fond of Anna Francis as a candidate, after all?"

"She had her strengths and her weaknesses. That was true of everyone we looked at," the secretary responded.

He pursed his lips and looked away.

KATJA

"You were the first to disappear from the house after Anna. Can you walk us through it?"

The lead interrogator put down his coffee cup, which the uniformed guard had brought in a moment before. They had just returned from a short break; Katja had gone to the bathroom while the second interrogator left the room to order coffee for all of them. Katja thought they looked tired, both the lead and the second interrogator. She wondered who they had spoken with already and who they had left on their list. She still didn't quite know why it was so important for them to get a clear picture of every detail, and above all she didn't know why the interrogations were taking place here, and performed by security officials. She understood that it meant something had gone wrong, but she didn't know what. Now here she was again, trying to remind herself to just answer the questions. It was harder than she'd expected; it seemed like extra information kept slipping out alongside what she meant to say. But this was a question she could answer.

"It was a fairly simple plan. We had a camera down on the Strategic Level; the images were sent to the screen of Henry's watch. The quality wasn't very good, of course, but we could at least keep track of where Anna was. Henry prepared the pier when he was searching that part of the island along with Franziska and Jon. They were occupied in the boathouse. I sneaked in before him and he came after me as soon as he had the chance. We staged a little fight together, and when Anna started to come up I lay down on the floor in a puddle of blood."

The lead interrogator nodded in agreement, as if these were facts he already knew, which he probably did.

"And what happened when she came up?"

"The hope was that she would turn around in the hatch and go right back down as soon as she saw me lying there, that she would assume I was dead. The point was for her to see me. That was all."

"But?" The lead interrogator urged her on in her story.

"Instead she came over to examine me. Henry had to take her out."

"Take her out?"

This was the second interrogator's question, and she put emphasis on each syllable. Katja cleared her throat.

"Yes, with a blow to the temple. There was no danger to her; he's a professional."

"You weren't worried about what consequences this might have to her health?"

The tone was mild, but her gaze had hardened.

"Like I said, he's a professional, and I'm a doctor. We were aware, of course, that this sort of situation might arise, and that this was a potential solution that wouldn't put Anna in any immediate danger."

The second interrogator bent over her papers and made a note. *Those notes. What is she writing?* Katja wondered again. The second interrogator went on, her eyes still on her papers.

"And once you had 'taken her out'?"

"We cleaned up, and I stopped to keep an eye on her until she showed the first signs of coming to. Then Henry left, I hid near the kitchen door, and when the others ran up from behind the house I left that way and made my way down to the underground shelter. And then I was out of play."

"Interesting. I would like to move on to another topic. Let's go back to the report you received earlier, before you arrived on the island. What more did you read about Anna Francis?"

"Well, there had been some sort of problem where she didn't obey orders."

"Can you expand on that?" the lead interrogator asked.

"She was ordered to stop negotiating with the military."

"And what happened?"

"She continued to negotiate, if I'm not mistaken. Behind the backs of her superiors. And they found out. And then there was some trouble."

"Trouble?"

"She was ordered to give in and stop negotiating once and for all. And then that situation arose . . ."

The lead interrogator nodded in encouragement. "Go on."

"When they went in to put a stop to the negotiations, in her place, the military attacked the medical transports. A lot of people died there in a short amount of time."

"And how do you know all of this?"

This was the second interrogator, intervening. For some reason, she made Katja more nervous than the lead interrogator. Her techniques were more difficult to defend oneself against.

"Anna's version of the incident is in the report. And so are her superiors'."

"What were the consequences?"

"It was probably around that point that she began to break down, and her use of FLL grew more serious, if I have understood it correctly. She just couldn't deal with it all, after that."

The second interrogator made another note and appeared to be pondering her next move; then she asked, "Would you say it was right or wrong of her to disobey orders?"

"That's not up to me to evaluate," Katja said quickly. *No speculation; just answer the questions.*

"They wanted to put her in front of a military tribunal. Send her home, even then, did you know that?"

"No."

Katja was about to say that perhaps they ought to have done so, so that Anna would have been spared all of this, but she pressed her lips together to stop herself from saying any more. The second interrogator held her gaze for a moment to see if she planned to expand upon her answer. Then she conferred in whispers with the lead interrogator as he paged through the papers in front of them, found what he was looking for, and handed it to her. The second interrogator took up the line of questioning again.

"Now I'd like to talk some more about what happened on the island. You were there to be in charge of the medical side of things. Would you say that your medical resources would have been sufficient to deal with severe trauma, such as gun-shot wounds?"

"No."

"Did you know that there was a gun on the island?"

Katja had not anticipated this question.

"No, I didn't know that."

"I see," said the second interrogator, without taking her eyes from Katja. "What would you have thought of this, had you been asked?"

"I would have said that it was profoundly inappropriate."

"What do you think about the fact that you weren't asked?"

Katja hesitated to answer. She was surprised to learn about the gun, but she tried once again to remind herself not to speculate about things that didn't pertain to her part of the narrative. At the same time, she knew she wouldn't get away with saying nothing. She tried to choose her words carefully.

"I was responsible for the medical situation on the island, as you yourself pointed out. I suppose I don't consider it within my area of responsibility to make that decision. But if you want my opinion, it sounds like it was a very bad idea."

"Why?" The second interrogator kept staring at her as if she were trying to hypnotize her.

"Well, you can never be certain what a person might do under extreme stress and isolation, can you? What anyone might do?"

"But if you were medically responsible, wouldn't you think it was your responsibility to make sure that the medical resources were sufficient to treat any injuries that might occur? Shouldn't you have known more?"

"One might think so."

"Do you think so?"

"I don't want to answer that question."

The second interrogator finally looked away from her and leaned back in her chair. At the same instant, the lead interrogator suddenly bent forward. He no longer looked as friendly. *They're good at this*, Katja thought. *They've had practice.*

"Okay. Let's return to what sort of information about Anna Francis you were given in advance. Is there anything else worth mentioning?"

Katja thought about what she should say. These constant jumps through time and changes of subject made her feel uncertain about what they were trying to get at with their questions, and what she had actually said. Presumably, she thought, that was the point.

"Yes."

"And what is that?"

"Well, it was that . . . I'm sorry, I find this very uncomfortable to talk about."

Katja took a breath. The lead interrogator urged her on.

"I understand, but we have to get to the bottom of what happened."

"Yes. Okay, it was about that shooting."

"Tell us what you knew."

"Well, she had fired a gun at a civilian in the hospital. I'm guessing that was why they sent her home, in the end."

"Who was this civilian?"

The lead interrogator's voice was low and neutral, but his body language revealed that he was focusing intensely. The second interrogator's eyes were fixed on her too.

"It was a boy from the village."

"What were the circumstances?"

"He had broken into the hospital that night. She thought it was someone trying to steal medicine."

"Medicine? Not FLL?" asked the second interrogator, who was also leaning across the table by this point.

"Well, it was probably all in the same place," Katja said, trying to remember what she had read in the report. *Why do I want to defend her?* she asked herself.

"But it wasn't true?"

"No, not as far as I know. He was looking for food. She shot the head off a ten-year-old boy who stole an apple."

The first interrogator gave her an ingratiating smile.

"Well, we're nearly finished! All that's left is a couple of questions to wrap up. I understand this is taxing, but we need to get a clear picture of all the details."

"Why is that?" Katja asked.

The lead interrogator gave no signs that he had heard her; instead he asked if she wanted a taxi and conveyed her wishes by way of the black telephone that was on the desk beside the tape recorder. Katja felt herself begin to relax. The second interrogator sat quietly, apparently looking through her notes. Without taking her eyes from them, she asked in a mild tone: "Did you know there was more than one candidate on the island?"

Katja was startled.

"What?"

"Did you know that?"

"No . . . I'm sorry, are you sure that's true?"

Katja's heart suddenly started pounding hard in her ears. *What was this?* Both interrogators were now looking directly at her, studying each of her reactions, as if they wanted to make sure they didn't miss a single hint about whether she was telling the truth or lying.

"Am I to interpret your response to mean that you did not know that?"

"No. I mean . . . correct. I didn't know that. Who was it?"

"Unfortunately, I am unable to say," said the second interrogator.

Katja gave a reflexive shake of her head.

"But . . . what happened to the second candidate?"

JON VON POST

"Now I'd like to jump forward to the final phase of the operation. Can we talk about that?"

Jon rubbed the sweat from his forehead; it had started to pour out of him again. The air in the room felt stuffy and poor.

He was sitting there in the bright room with the dark windows and sweating. His knees ached. Across from him sat a woman and a man in their forties, the lead and second interrogators, like a pair of siblings. What they had gone through thus far was an endless series of details. When had he learned what? Who had said that? Could he recall if this thing or that had happened first? He responded to the best of his ability, his impatience growing. The Chairman had said it was necessary for him to do this, so he was doing it. He didn't have to like it.

The first interrogator turned to the woman and whispered something in her ear, at which she nodded, located a folder on the table, and handed it to him. The lead interrogator paged through it for a moment, then put it down on the table and awaited Jon's reply.

"If we truly must."

The lead interrogator tilted his head.

"It sounds like you'd rather not?"

"I just don't feel like it."

"Why do you find this difficult?"

This was the woman, the second interrogator, asking, as if she hadn't heard what he'd said. Or was ignoring it.

"Why would I want to go through all that crap again? Did you know I haven't slept through the night since I got home from that goddamn island? You ruined me. You must be aware of that, right? That you ruin people?"

"We are very grateful for your cooperation," the lead interrogator declared mechanically. Each time Jon raised any objection, the response had been similar. He went on: "It is important for us to understand what happened on the island. So can we discuss the final phase of the operation now?"

"Yes. May I have some water?"

The second interrogator took the carafe and poured a glass to hand to him.

"Can't you ask Lotte about this instead?" Jon asked after taking a sip.

"Lotte Colliander is exempt from these interrogations. She will report directly to the Chairman now that she is a member of his staff," the lead interrogator replied. The second interrogator shot him a look of irritation; it seemed she thought he was saying too much. Without a word, Jon handed the glass back for a refill. The lead interrogator poured more water into it, simultaneously asking, "How did you receive your instructions from Henry Fall?"

Jon took the glass and drained it in three gulps before answering.

"So he came into my room and confirmed his identity as an agent again. There was more to tell than what he'd said down in the kitchen, so he explained the situation, told me that he had drugged Lotte . . . that is, to keep her from having a breakdown, and he said he would soon be moving her to the shelter behind the house where the others were waiting. He told me to walk down a path, around the house, through the brambles, along the rock wall, and into the underground shelter below the north-western corner of the house. He said Anna was the one being tested, not us, and that she was alive. But the situation had become precarious now that he didn't know where the gun was, and we had to get to safety as soon as possible. He asked me to go on ahead, by way of the stairs to the kitchen at the end of the hall, and then take the kitchen door out to the back. He would follow with Lotte very soon after; he just had to gather his things."

"And how did you react to that?" the lead interrogator wondered.

"I did as he said. What else could I do?"

"So you believed him," the lead interrogator wanted to confirm. Jon considered this.

"Yes, it seemed plausible. Or at least, it wasn't any less plausible than anything else about the situation. And of course it was a relief to hear that Franziska . . . or, I mean, the others, hadn't been harmed."

It felt strange to say Franziska's name. He had tried to contact her a number of times since the island but always received the same response. That she was busy, and later on, that she had traveled out of the country "to recuperate." He wondered what that meant. He hadn't seen her on TV a single time since Isola. He'd asked the interrogators about this earlier, but they said more or less the same thing: she was "resting up" after her experiences on the island. Presumably her brother-in-law was protecting her; if you were family of the Minister of the Interior, you probably didn't have to sit for interrogations if you didn't want to.

"So you made your way to the underground shelter. How was the mood there?"

"Pretty calm. Franziska had arrived just a few hours earlier, the same way. And, you know, the whole thing was pretty surreal."

"What do you mean?"

"Well, it was like Judgment Day. People you thought were dead. And then they were just sitting there."

Jon shuddered internally. He remembered the peculiar sensation in the underground shelter. How the others had stared at him in the dimly lit little room. How it had felt like they were all uncertain whether they were dead or alive. How he still woke up at night and wasn't quite sure.

"We're very nearly finished here," said the second interrogator. "Just one more thing. Henry spoke with you about his assignment two times. Both you and Lotte were there the first time, but the second time was in your room, right?" Jon nodded. The second interrogator continued.

"How did Henry Fall present himself when he gave you the information in your room?"

"He said he was an intelligence officer and he was charged with watching over Anna and protecting her."

"Nothing more?" The second interrogator looked at him, eyebrows raised.

"No," Jon replied. "Was there more to it?"

THE SECRETARY

Now IT WAS the second interrogator's turn again. She shuffled the papers in front of her as if she were looking for something.

"Will this be much longer?" the secretary asked, casting an annoyed glance at his wrist although he no longer had a watch on it.

"That is entirely up to you," she responded without looking at him.

"I would like some coffee," he said, and he could tell that he sounded like a whiny child. She pretended not to hear him; instead she started in from another direction.

"So at which point did you all decide to have two candidates? Both Henry Fall and Anna Francis?"

The secretary swallowed. His mouth felt dry. He really would have liked some coffee.

"I understood all along that this operation was far too large and risky to put all our hopes on a single candidate."

"Was that everyone's understanding?"

"What do you mean?"

"Was everyone made aware that there were two candidates on the island?"

The secretary tried to work out what she was really asking, but he couldn't.

"What are you trying to get at?" he asked.

The second interrogator shoved all her documents together until they were in a perfect stack before she spoke again.

"Okay, I'll phrase it like this: Was the Chairman informed that you had placed two potential candidates on the island? Both Anna Francis and Henry Fall?"

The secretary felt the air grow heavier in the room as it might just before a thunderstorm.

"That's a silly question," he said. "I don't understand what you're trying to suggest."

The second interrogator looked at him. Her little smile was gone.

"Please just answer the question," said the lead interrogator, as if to remind them that he was still there too.

"Yes, of course I informed the Chairman. Why would I make that sort of decision on my own?"

"The Chairman," the second interrogator drawled, "says he had no idea that you had a second candidate on the island. He thought Henry Fall was one of the people who would test Anna Francis."

The secretary couldn't believe his ears.

"What?"

She began again as if he truly hadn't heard her.

"The Chairman says he didn't know . . ."

The secretary rose from the table. His whole body was trembling.

"What the hell is this? What are you saying? Turn off that goddamn tape recorder!"

Without a word, and with the satisfied expression of a person who has just bowled a strike, the second interrogator bent toward the tape recorder and switched it off.

A LITTLE WHILE later she bent over again and pressed "record."

"Interrogation resumed. Now let's return to the question of whether you had informed the Chairman of the plan to put more than one candidate on the island."

The secretary was speaking quickly, tripping over his words.

"I misunderstood the question earlier. The answer is no, I made the decision to place more candidates on the island all on my own. I regarded it as within my sphere of authority to make such a decision without informing the Chairman."

"Did anyone other than you know who the second candidate was?"

At this point, the questions were coming directly from the second interrogator.

"No one but those under me. Very few people."

She put out her hand, and the lead interrogator handed her a folder. She didn't take her eyes from the secretary. Her pupils were large and black. *She smells blood,* he thought.

"Some documents exist," said the second interrogator, "in which you confirm that there is a second candidate, and you also mention that second candidate by name. If this was in fact an official decision, then how come you didn't inform the Chairman? Didn't it seem appropriate to go up the ladder for support when it came to such a crucial decision?"

"Like I said, I misunderstood your earlier question; I thought you meant to ask if I *ought to* have informed the Chairman. Of course I should have done so. But I didn't."

"Was Henry Fall himself aware? That he was a candidate?"

"No," said the secretary. "Neither Anna Francis nor Henry Fall knew that they themselves were the ones being tested for placement in the RAN group. But Henry knew Anna was a candidate. He knew that she hadn't died that first night, that she was alive."

"And what was the plan, having two candidates on the island?"

"Well, it was simply to see which of them was best equipped to handle the situation."

"And how was that to be determined?"

"It was to be evaluated afterward."

The second interrogator raised her eyebrows again. The secretary wanted to slam a brick into those fucking eyebrows.

"In what way would it be evaluated afterward?" she asked.

"Well, what usually happens? We would walk through the situation, listen to their reports. Look at the answer key, so to speak. Nothing sensational. Standard procedure." The secretary tried to maintain the same mild tone that the second interrogator employed, but he could tell that his voice sounded alarmingly shrill.

"Was that all?"

"Yes, of course. Do you have differing information?" he said before he could stop himself.

"So it is not true that you said, and I quote, 'We'll see which of them gets off the island alive'?"

By this point, cold sweat was running down the secretary's back. He could see where this was heading. *He's sacrificing me*, he thought. *That goddamn Chairman is actually going to sacrifice me this time.* He thought back to the meetings he'd had with the Chairman before the interrogations commenced. "It will look better if you're the one who takes the fall, but naturally it's all just for appearances; eventually you'll be exonerated. I'm behind you one hundred percent." Hadn't he looked a little odd even then? Hadn't he avoided meeting the secretary's gaze? The secretary realized that he had been stupid. That he had been gullible. And now he was on his own.

"Who claims I said that?"

"Just answer the question—did you say that?"

"I don't recall."

"You don't recall?"

"I don't recall. I talk a lot. I might have been joking. Not everyone understands my sense of humor."

The second interrogator made a little face. She looked down at her papers and jotted down another note.

"Whose idea was it to place the gun on the island?" the lead interrogator suddenly interjected.

"Don't recall," the secretary hurried to repeat.

"Did you tell Henry Fall to bring a gun?"

"Don't recall."

The lead interrogator stretched. "Mr. Secretary," he said in an authoritative voice, "I must remind you of the gravity of this situation. One of the candidates you selected for evaluation under extreme conditions, the highly valued security officer Henry Fall, is now in the morgue. The other candidate is in the hospital after attempting to take her own life. The result of this 'evaluation,' as you call it, cannot be described as anything but a complete disaster, both ethically and strategically. Someone will have to take responsibility for this incident. Do you understand what I'm saying? It will not suffice to plead memory loss in this instance."

"No, and it is absolutely regrettable, but I truly don't remember every word and action."

The second interrogator looked up. She put the papers down on the table and leaned toward him.

"How about if I pose the question like this," she said slowly. "Was it part of your plan that only one of them would leave the island alive? Was that, in fact, the test?"

The secretary leaned forward as well. There were only a few inches separating their faces. In a low voice, he said: "You can ask as many times as you want. I have only one response: the only thing I did was try to take responsibility for the security of the Union. Can you say the same for yourselves?"

The second interrogator did not take her eyes from him. She opened her mouth to say something but then closed it again.

"You've been fooled too," the secretary whispered to the second interrogator. "Don't you get it? He fooled all of us."

"Mr. Secretary," said the lead interrogator, "I must remind you that this is . . ."

Suddenly the secretary leaned backward and crossed his arms over his chest; his prison shirt formed a small crease over his breastbone.

"I won't respond to any further questions. Take me back to my cell."

The second interrogator reached for the tape recorder, leaned forward, and said:

"Interrogation concluded."

THE END

(OR THE BEGINNING)

ANNA

I WAS AWAKENED by birdsong. The room was white. Something was sparkling and dangling before my eyes, and when I tried to focus on it I realized it was that handle thing that hangs above hospital beds, to make it easier for debilitated people to sit up. The sun glittered on the chain, which was swinging back and forth a little as if it had just been used. I slowly turned my head. At the edge of the bed sat the Chairman; he was paging through a women's magazine. I wondered how long he had been sitting there and how long I had been asleep. Or whatever it's called. I had been given so many sleeping pills that I hardly knew whether it was sleep or an induced coma. They didn't want to take any risks, they said. I needed rest, they said. They didn't want me to kill myself, they didn't say, but I assumed that was what they actually meant. The question was whether that was what I wanted. I didn't know.

I tried to move a little. It was slow going; my arms didn't quite want to obey.

"Anna? Are you awake?"

The Chairman put down the magazine and leaned forward with a fatherly smile.

"Can I have some water?"

He stood up, walked over to the sink near the door, and filled a plastic cup with water. I followed him with my eyes; he came back to the bed and handed me the cup, then sat back down on the chair.

"I thought it was about time to come look in on you myself."

I let my gaze drift beyond his head, out the window, which was open a crack despite the bars. White clouds moving across a blue sky. I thought of the last time I had seen clouds moving so rapidly across the sky, and realized it was with Henry, behind the house. The memory caused my body to stiffen with discomfort. The Chairman looked at me and said in a kind voice:

"You should know that we're worried about you."

Just as I started to wonder what he meant by "we," he went on: "Those of us with the RAN project, of course, but above all, your family. Your mother and daughter. They need you. They don't want to lose you. We don't either."

I swallowed. My mouth felt dry, so I took a sip of water from the plastic cup. There was a wilted bouquet of flowers at the foot of the bed; next to it was a card on which Siri had written "Get better soon, Mom," in carefully printed little-kid letters. I wondered what they had told her was wrong with me. I hoped they hadn't told her the truth. I turned to the Chairman.

"Why are you here?"

He hesitated for a moment.

"Why am I here . . . ? Well, I wanted to see how you're do-ing, of course, with my own eyes, so to speak."

He gestured toward a big box of chocolates on the win-dowsill, one of those gold, expensive ones with the portrait of the Minister on it. I wondered if the Chairman dreamed of a box of chocolates with his own face on it. I looked at him, sit-ting there in that ever-present suit. Judging from his expres-sion, my health was not the only reason that he was at my bedside. I didn't say anything, just kept looking at him, until he began to speak again.

"I think it's time someone sat down with you for some straight talk, to explain the situation. All of this tiptoeing around and coddling you—I think it's only making things worse. The doctors think you need it, but I believe you're tougher than that. I believe . . ."

He took a deep breath. There was something self-righteous about his tone that both irked me and made me feel suspicious.

"I believe that the only way to help you heal is to be com-pletely honest. With you and with ourselves. I believe there are things you need to know about and take into consider-ation when it comes time to make decisions about your fu-ture. Do you understand what I'm saying?"

I nodded.

"Okay then. Do you think you know enough about what happened on Isola and what went wrong?"

I nodded. Yes, I had read the report; it was absolutely unbearable.

"Then I would also like to ask, personally and honestly, for your forgiveness. As you know there are many things that should not have happened, and although I am ultimately responsible as the director, I would still like to emphasize that the secretary has admitted that he acted on his own authority, without informing his superiors as procedure dictates. He will be prosecuted for this. Yes—it was decided that Henry should be there to watch over you. It was not, however, officially decided that he should bring a gun. Nor was it decided that he was a second candidate, nor was it on my initiative that FLL was present on the island. The fact that these things did happen is of course my own fault in some respects, in that the person who made these unfortunate decisions was directly under me, but I want to assure you that it was never my intent for things to turn out the way they did."

I looked at him.

"Bullshit."

He was startled.

"What do you mean?"

"Are you really telling me that the secretary did all of this on his own? Without informing you? 'I knew nothing.' Of course you knew all of this; you're just disappointed that it went to hell, because now you have to clean up the mess."

The Chairman leaned back in his chair and held up his hand as if to stop me. His lips had narrowed into a grim line.

"Let me say first of all that I am happy to see you have recovered some of your old spunk, although naturally I am hurt that you don't have greater trust in me. But I suppose it's understandable, in its own way. But let's get back to the straight talk. I'm here because I want to offer you the job."

"Excuse me?"

I thought I must have misheard.

"Just what I said. We have evaluated you under the most

extreme of circumstances, and, given your background, I still consider the decisions you made to be well motivated throughout. The price was high, sure, but we're all in agreement that you handled the situation with just the type of resolve and rationality it demanded."

I couldn't believe my ears. It felt like there was a volcano inside me, a sudden rage that had been slumbering in my chest; it welled up with an unforeseen power.

"What the hell are you talking about? I shot my friend! He was innocent!" I screamed. And then came the tears. The tears that had been dammed up since the moment I began to suspect that something was terribly wrong, the moment those two military helicopters landed. One beside me, the other on the other side of the island. Paramedics hurried out; two of them wrapped me in a blanket and gave me something to drink. I tried to tell them that Henry was in the house, but they were already heading in with stretchers and medical bags. I shouted, but what came out was so incoherent that they didn't seem to understand me at all. "Drink, drink up. You need to get warm" was all they said.

Suddenly I started to think about the other helicopter. What was it doing behind the house? I didn't understand. At that moment, someone came out of the house, supported by two paramedics. It was Lotte. I hurled myself up to run over to her. The paramedics caught me and held me down. I tried to call out to her, but she just stared at me with dim, blank eyes as she stumbled off toward the back of the house with a paramedic under each arm.

"She's alive! She's alive!"

I was hysterical with delight even as my overcooked brain

couldn't figure out how this could be. My head was a jumble of various impulses; I saw soldiers and paramedics running around the island as if in a movie, and I didn't really understand what was going on or why.

Then I saw the second helicopter sail up into the sky from behind the house. It had an open cockpit and it was full of people. I saw the colonel. The wind was whipping at his hair and he raised his hand as if in a greeting, but the helicopter veered away before I could respond; it headed toward the mainland. I grabbed the collar of one of the paramedics holding on to me, pulled him down, and screamed straight into his face:

"Why are they alive?"

"Anna, you have to take it easy. You're in bad shape. We have to get you out of here."

At that instant I saw something else. More paramedics were carrying a stretcher down from the house. A stretcher that was completely draped. The way you do with people who are definitely dead. People who have been shot in the head. I didn't understand what it meant, how this had happened or why, but suddenly it was like I understood anyway. Like window blinds opening and revealing the whole picture, in all its beauty and horror. I suddenly understood what I had done and what I needed to do.

I took a deep breath, let it out, and made my whole body relax. I felt the paramedics' grip loosen. Then I breathed in again, as deep as I could, wrenched myself out of their grasp, ran for the edge of the cliff, and threw myself over it.

I remembered all of this, as one does, in a single image and full of tiny details at the same time. After the cliff there were only tiny images, like the individual frames of a film. A hospital corridor with lights on the ceiling. A needle in my arm. A cervical collar holding my head still. An operating table. A blurry view of Nour and Siri through a pane of glass. A nurse changing a cast. A scalpel someone had set aside on an examination table. A bathroom. Blood, blood, blood. More needles in my arms. Fresh bandages. Straps around my arms. Sleep, darkness. Someone changing my pillow. Worried voices speaking softly. Someone giving me pills. Someone checking under my tongue to make sure I actually swallowed the pills. Someone forcing me to swallow them. Periods of unbearable wakefulness and clarity. More sleep, more darkness. And then, today, birdsong. And the Chairman at my bedside. I remembered all of this as I sat there in my bed. What started as trickling tears soon turned into sobbing unlike anything I had experienced before. It was as if my entire body were crying, and it came from an ancient place so deep inside me that I had never been aware of it. The Chairman made no move to comfort me; he just sat there and let me cry. Eventually my tears ebbed away.

"Can we continue?" the Chairman asked in a low voice. I nodded.

"Then I would like to get back to laying out the conditions for you. The job is yours if you want it. Before you decide to decline the offer, I'd like you to listen to the alternatives. This job is a permanent position with the RAN group. Your work will be classified, and I believe you will come to find it both rewarding and extremely demanding. You will never want for anything, when it comes to the material side of things. The amount I mentioned as compensation for the Isola assignment will be your yearly salary. Your daughter will be able to attend the best schools. We'll destroy the old reports on your mother. We will provide any necessities you and your family could possibly need: housing, transport, during both working hours and vacation time. You will not be working all the time. There may be weeks and months when we don't need you. During those periods, you will have time off with full pay. But you will always be on duty. When we need you, you come. It will be trying sometimes, but it won't be any worse than what you've already experienced. Does that sound reasonable?"

I nodded mutely. The Chairman went on in his low voice, his eyes on the door as if he wanted to make sure no one would come in and interrupt us.

"Anyway. If you choose to decline this offer, then I must inform you that, unfortunately, what awaits on the other side of the balance is not particularly pleasant. The fact is, you will no longer be in our employ and as such you will not enjoy the immunity of the Union, which means that you can expect to be prosecuted for homicide or manslaughter of your former colleague Henry Fall. This is a pity, of course, but there is nothing I can do about it. You may certainly hire a lawyer, someone who can do their best in court, but I would say that the evidence against you is overwhelming and your chance of going free is minimal. Perhaps you can claim extenuating cir-cumstances and plead your sentence down to a fixed prison sentence instead of life or the death penalty. Maybe ten years. Maybe less, maybe more. How old is your daughter, by the way?"

He looked at me. I said nothing. He went on: "I must also stress that if you take your own life, your daughter will not only lose a parent, she will also lose everything in her possession. It is a crime against the state to commit suicide when you are facing indictment. Obstruction of justice, it's called, and it is punishable by seizure of property, which extends to surviving relatives. This is a relic from the days of Cold War II, and it is seldom put into practice, but in this case it would certainly be appropriate. We would also have to examine how familiar your mother was with your views, and we might need to go back through her old files and consider the reasons she left the party."

The Chairman fixed his eyes on me. "Do you understand what I'm saying?"

His hand searched his jacket pocket and took something from it. *It's a gun—he's going to shoot me*, I thought. But it wasn't. It was two envelopes, and he tossed them on the blanket before me.

"One is your employment contract; the other is a detention order. Your choice."

I didn't look at him; I didn't look at the envelopes—instead I looked at the wilted bouquet at the foot of the bed. It wasn't really much of a bouquet, more a bundle of grass and leaves. I knew that Siri must have picked it herself, probably in Nour's courtyard, where weeds blossomed between the cobblestones, where Nour liked to put out a few pots and try to grow tomatoes, even though it was too cold and shady and they failed every year. Nour's rough hands growing older and older, more wrinkled and trembling; hands that might not manage very much longer, hands that dug in the dirt alongside Siri's small soft ones, black rinds of dirt under their thin nails. Her hands had been so tiny when she was a baby, round as stuffed cushions, little dimples at the knuckles. Her hands around my finger, in my hair. Her heart against mine. Nothing between them. Now her hands were thin and strong. But they were still small. They were still awfully small.

And suddenly I understood. I understood everything.

"Anna? I'd like to hear how you feel about all of this. Which envelope will it be? Do you accept the offer?"

"There was no test."

My own voice sounded like a stranger's, dry and creaky. The Chairman was perfectly silent. He didn't move; he stood absolutely still. I continued:

"There never was any test, was there? Not of me or anyone else. Because if there had been one, I would have failed on all fronts. So there wasn't one. It was a trap. You've got me exactly where you want me. You wanted me to have no choice. You wanted me to take this job; I don't understand why you want me, but there it is. But you knew I would never under any circumstances accept it willingly, so you put me in a situation in which I would have no other choice. And you got rid of the secretary while you were at it. I don't know why you wanted to do that either, but I'm sure you have your reasons. Now you can lock him up for the rest of his life. Poof, he's gone."

I gave a laugh. It sounded strange. The Chairman still hadn't moved a muscle. All I could hear was my own breathing.

"But there's one thing I don't understand. Why did you want to get rid of Henry? What did he ever do to you?"

I waited for the Chairman to say something, although I was aware that I wouldn't receive an answer. After a long silence, the Chairman spoke in a mild tone.

"That's certainly an interesting theory. And maybe some

of your questions will be answered eventually, what do I know? And there certainly may be reasons why the RAN group needs you in particular, reasons I can't discuss with you at the moment, but which might come to light in good time. *If you accept my offer, that is.* Otherwise, of course, you will never know. So now, Anna, I would like to ask for your response. What will it be?"

I looked the Chairman straight in the eye. His pupils were wide and black. Deep down inside them I caught a glimpse of a cold, surreal, and terrifying madness. I really had no choice. Somehow I had known all along that it would end like this. So I nodded at the Chairman. That was that.

His face split into a brilliant smile; he picked up the other envelope, stuck it back in his inner pocket, and put out his right hand.

"Excellent! Anna Francis—I would like to extend a warm welcome to the RAN group."

STOCKHOLM

THE PROTECTORATE OF SWEDEN

MARCH 2037

HENRY

"I'M SORRY, BUT I don't quite understand what it is I'm supposed to do. What is this all about?"

The secretary took out an envelope and handed it to me. I gave him a curious look and he nodded at the envelope.

"Open it."

I opened the envelope and took out a folder made of stiff paper; when I turned it over, a familiar face was staring up at me from a copy of a passport that was fastened to the upper left-hand corner. It was Anna Francis.

"She's our candidate," said the secretary. "Your job is to watch over her and protect her."

I looked at him. I didn't know what to say.

"It won't be that difficult. She'll be dead for the better part of the time. Or at least, that's what everyone will think. Everyone but you and another trusted participant."

I looked down at the picture of Anna. The picture must have been taken by a photographer, because she didn't look like herself. She looked beautiful in a doctored sort of way, as if she had been relieved of her soul. I tried to think—which question was the right one to ask now?

"How will this all transpire?"

"She will go underground by way of a staged murder. Then you will take out the others."

He noticed my expression.

"No—that is, not for real; but to her it must look like the others are disappearing one by one. We want to see what she does, how she acts, what sorts of weaknesses she shows. Above all, we want to make sure she is capable of sticking to an order, of not revealing herself, even though everything will suggest that she ought to do the opposite. We want to give her a stress test, is the long and short of it."

This all seemed incredibly strange. I tried to gather my thoughts and figure out how it would work. The secretary was giving me an expectant look, as if he assumed I would have questions.

"So . . . in the end, she and I are the only ones left. What do I do then?"

"Then you may tell her what's going on, if you like. But not before."

A thought struck me.

"She's going to think I'm the murderer if she and I are the only ones left. What if she doesn't believe me, no matter what I say?"

"That's why it's so important for *you* to be there. She trusts you, if I'm not mistaken. You know her; you know how she thinks. She likes you, I've heard."

I wondered where he had heard that, but I didn't ask. The secretary seemed to be able to tell I wasn't following.

"Did you ever play Wink Murder when you were little?"

I shook my head. The secretary began to explain: "It goes like this: One person is randomly chosen as a murderer and another is the detective. The other players, the victims, know who the detective is, but they don't know the murderer. Then everyone walks around the room. The murderer kills people by discreetly winking at them. When someone gets blinked at, they fall down dead. When the detective thinks he knows who the murderer is, he accuses the suspect. If the detective is right, he wins; if not, the murderer wins."

The secretary stuck his knife into the salmon on his plate. It was so pink, almost raw inside. I suddenly had the sense that he was cutting into a newborn.

"Perfect," the secretary said with a contented sigh. He didn't take his eyes from the plate. "It's really no more difficult than that. You can think of this little exercise as a version of Wink Murder."

He stuck the pink salmon in his mouth and appeared to swallow it without chewing. I cleared my throat.

"No, I've never played that game. Have you?"

The secretary looked up at me. His gray eyes sparkled.

"It was my favorite game."